The
Golden
Venture

Also by
JANE FLORY

The
Golden
Venture

By JANE FLORY

Houghton Mifflin Company Boston 1976

J
c. 2

Library of Congress Cataloging in Publication Data

Flory, Jane, 1917-
   The golden venture.

   SUMMARY: Determined to accompany her father
to the California gold fields, a young girl stows
away in one of the westward bound wagons and finds
herself involved in an adventure that requires all
her wits and emotional resources.
   [1. California—Gold discoveries—Fiction.
2. Frontier and pioneer life—Fiction] I. Title.
PZ7.F665Go   [Fic]   75-43899
ISBN 0-395-24377-7

CL SEP '76

1

MINNIE WELDON and her best friend walked slowly home from school, enjoying the pale spring sunshine and not saying much in particular. Annamary said idly, "Nice to have St. Joseph quiet for a change. Pa says the gold rush has been good for business, but I got awful tired of the crowds."

"Well, they're off now. Maybe a few more to leave, but they'll have to hurry if they're to get over the mountains before the first snow falls. That's what my father says. He says if that crazy mob doesn't move fast, they'll be caught in the drifts."

With spring just barely there, it was hard to think ahead to next winter when snow would fall early on those faraway mountain passes they had heard so much about. St. Joseph, Missouri, was weeks and months away from those mountains that had proved to be so treacherous for unwary gold-seekers.

The pioneers in the earlier wagons that had made their last civilized stop in St. Joseph were homemakers, farmers, who were better prepared for the hardships that lay ahead of them. Most of them had studied maps and made careful lists of the provisions and tools they would need for the trip west to find a new home.

But the would-be goldminers were different. When the first news of gold in California came in 1849, otherwise sensible people lost their heads. With only the vaguest idea of what they would have to go through, they impulsively decided to go clear across the country and get their share of the fabled gold. Some of them came in flimsy wagons or buggies with a few bags of food and no warm clothing. They left homes and jobs in a frenzy of gold madness, gathered up a shovel or a pickaxe and ran to be the first to pick up the huge gold nuggets they expected to find. One man trundled through St. Joseph with all his belongings heaped on a hand cart.

"Pa tried to tell them," said Minnie. "He tried and tried, but most of them just wouldn't listen. He says there'll be a trail of bones from here to California, and not all of them animal bones, either."

Annamary shuddered. "I'm glad my father runs a store. He'll sell them provisions, but he says those goldminers couldn't pay him to go along. Not for a thousand dollars, even."

Minnie nodded. "I wouldn't mind seeing the country, but not the way they're doing it. Our mules and horses are strung out all across the country. Pa supplied them for many a wagon, but you wouldn't catch him leaving a good livery stable to chase after gold. Let's go home by way of the stable."

Annamary agreed. The livery stable was a pleasant place to visit. Mr. Weldon was always glad to see Minnie and her friends, no matter how busy he was. Minnie's Aunt Addie didn't like to have her hang around there, but Minnie solved that by just not telling her. Father didn't allow bad language or rough talk around his place, and he said there was no harm in a little visit on the way home from school.

St. Joseph was a busy town, but it wasn't a big town at all, and the trip home from school was a short one no matter which street they took. The livery stable was not far out of their way and neither girl was in a hurry.

Mr. Weldon was there, loading a big farm wagon that stood just inside the open doors. He heaved a barrel of flour over the tail gate of the wagon, and stopped to mop his perspiring face.

"Howdy, Minnie, Annamary. How are my girls this fine day? Sun feels good, doesn't it?"

"It certainly does. Spring is here, all right, and the new grass is coming up. Whose wagon is that, Pa? Some slowpoke miner, I'll bet, bound for the West. He'd better move on out or he'll be too late."

Mr. Weldon's helper, Addison Tinker, laughed. "He's a slowpoke, all right, but he'll be moving out soon."

"Didn't trust the other miners, did he? Left his wagon here where it'd be safe, I guess. Where are his horses?"

Pa was busy loading another barrel. "Around

3

someplace. Maybe he'll be wanting a team from me. Want an apple?"

The girls each accepted an apple and sat on barrels in the sunshine to eat them. Minnie swung her feet as she crunched. "It'll soon be time for bare feet. I can't wait until Aunt Addie says I can take off my shoes. She hates bare feet, though. Says it's uncivilized."

Mr. Tinker laughed again. "Poor Miss Addie. She's got an uphill job keeping you and Pierce civilized out here in St. Joseph."

Minnie agreed. "She keeps working at it, though. Aunt Addie never gives up. She'll keep at it until I'm as civilized as a girl back East, civilized as a Philadelphian."

They all grinned. There was no malice in the remarks about Minnie's Aunt Addie, her mother's older sister. It was just that everyone in St. Joseph knew Miss Adeline Hunter, out from Philadelphia eleven years ago. She never let anyone forget that she had been used to the cultured life of a large city, and that St. Joseph was very rough and ready in comparison.

St. Joseph didn't care. It went on in its easy pleasant way, content to be one of the last towns on the frontier. After St. Joe and the Missouri River there were only miles and miles and miles of prairie and mountains and deserts, with occasional army outposts hundreds of miles apart. From St. Joseph to California, almost no human habitation in between. Nothing but the hundreds of miles of trail that led to the West Coast.

"I do have to go," said Annamary. "Today's wash day and I have to help take down the clothes and fold them so Ma can iron tomorrow."

"Me, too," said Minnie. She jumped down from her barrel and tossed her apple core away into the tall dried grass. Maybe in the long warm sunshiny days to come it would sprout and grow into an apple tree beside the livery stable. She knew she was expected home, but it was so nice outside, so peaceful. She listened for one last minute to the familiar sounds of Pa and Mr. Tinker talking, of the horses stamping in their stalls, of the new young horse, not yet broken, kicking now and then at the back wall. It was so much more inviting there than it would be at home.

Reluctantly she called good-bye to her father and Mr. Tinker and set off with Annamary. Her friend turned off three houses down Main Street from the Weldon's sturdy frame house. They both said, "See you in the morning," and Minnie went on her way. St. Joseph was full of nice sturdy frame houses. It was a sturdy well-built town. Nobody was very rich and no one was terribly poor. But the Weldon house was different from all the rest. Not a big difference, maybe, but it was there, even if you couldn't quite put your finger on it. For one thing, there was a neat brick walk leading up to the front door, instead of a grassy path. That was Aunt Addie's doing. She missed Philadelphia's red brick sidewalks, so Pa had ordered a load of bricks out from the East and laid them herringbone fashion to please her. She was pleased, too, although she did a lot of carrying on about Fools and their Money.

Then, too, the front door looked used and welcoming. Other people used their front doors only for the minister's calls or for funerals. For everything else, visitors showed up at the back door. But Aunt Addie disliked that habit.

"That's what a door is for," she said. "For coming and going. In Philadelphia no one calls at the back door except tradesmen. It's — it's hayseed!"

When Aunt Addie said something, she said it firmly, as if that was *that*. And nobody likes to be considered hayseed. So neighbors came to the front door at the Weldon house. They never caught Aunt Addie with the parlor undusted or the floors unpolished. She was the first woman to get her wash out on the clothesline Monday morning, the first one to have her flat irons heating on the stove on Tuesday. Wednesday was for a thorough housecleaning, much more elaborate than the housecleaning that went on each day. Thursday she mended and sewed, polished glass and silverware and, weather permitting, aired quilts and blankets. Friday she did the marketing and on Saturday she baked enough bread for the week, and all the cakes and cookies and puddings. In between all this she worked in the vegetable garden in season and visited the sick and sewed for the Missionary Society.

Sunday was the day for church, morning and

evening, and then rest for them all. No work at all, except for the work Aunt Addie did to get a magnificent Sabbath dinner on the table. No sewing, or playing with dolls, or hopscotch scratched into the dusty street, or singing, except for hymns. Only books of an uplifting nature were allowed. Father liked to read the weekly newspaper on Sunday to catch up with the news, but Aunt Addie forbid it. Sunday was a hard day to get through, bad enough in the winter when the weather was mean, but almost impossible in the spring and summer when all outdoors was calling and the wide Missouri rolled past sparkling in the sunshine.

Pa had to feed and water the horses even on Sunday, and Minnie knew he stretched out feeding time as long as he could. He took the paper along and read it back in his little office, and read books that he wanted to read even if they weren't uplifting. Aunt Addie wasn't fooled, but she couldn't do much about it. After all, in practically every other way, Pierce Weldon was a good man. Everyone said so, and Aunt Addie always said so herself. She said her dear late sister's husband was a very good man, although he was much too easygoing for his own welfare. But even for good men the enforced Sabbath rest day stretched out endlessly. Pierce Weldon and his daughter were always glad when the Sunday evening service was over and it was time to go to bed. On Monday a new week of activity would begin, and they could escape to the livery stable and get away from Aunt Addie's constant orders.

Minnie went around to the back yard. The clotheslines were bare. Aunt Addie had taken the wash in, too impatient to wait for Minnie to get home and do her Monday chores. Oh well, maybe she was in time to fold and dampen things, to make ready for the ironing tomorrow. It was not that she was so crazy about taking down clothes that made her sigh in disappointment. It was the lecture she knew she would get from Aunt Addie. She sighed again and went in the back door.

"Wipe your feet, Minnie," called her aunt.

"I already did, Aunt Addie."

"Your cookies and milk are there on the cupboard," said Aunt Addie over her shoulder as she bustled around, folding and separating the basket of laundry.

"What kept you so long? You know you are expected home promptly, Minnie. You have certain responsibilities, and you can't develop strength of character by shirking your responsibilities. Don't put your schoolbooks there, child, where you'll forget them. Put them on the hall table. It's been a beautiful day, hasn't it? I got twice as much wash done today, they blew dry so fast. I did all the big tablecloths. They were clean, of course, but linen does yellow if it isn't used constantly. Remember that when you have your own home, Minnie. Wash all the tablecloths often, whether they need it or not, and let the sun bleach them. Snowy tablecloths are the sign of a good housekeeper."

Aunt Addie was small, lively, always busy at

something, always on the go. One of her favorite sayings was "The Devil makes work for idle hands." Her hands were never idle, and that was fine with Minnie and her father, but she insisted that no one else should have idle hands either. Pierce and Minnie Weldon were much alike, and quite different from Miss Adeline Hunter. They could work hard when it was necessary but they both needed time for quiet and daydreaming and reading. There was nothing Aunt Addie scorned like daydreaming or anything else she considered frivolous. There was nothing frivolous about her. Her dark hair was pulled back firmly into a tight neat bun. No wisps were allowed to escape. Her house dresses were plain and businesslike and her aprons were always spotless, starched so stiff they could stand alone. Pierce Weldon sometimes grumbled that that was Miss Addie's trouble.

"She's spent too long over the starch kettle. Some of it got into her spine and now she can't bend at all. She's as stiff as her aprons."

In the short time it had taken Minnie to finish her milk and cookies her aunt had sprinkled and rolled all the clothes and was beginning now to prepare supper. She pumped a basin of water with the same energy she did everything else, and started to peel potatoes, her fingers flying.

"I'm glad the gold rush is over for this season," she said. "Now your father can come home on time for his supper. I guess the miners are all gone."

"There's at least one left. He's storing his wagon

9

at the stable — I saw it." Too late, Minnie realized she had given herself away. She hurried on to distract her aunt.

"It's a good big wagon. Pa was helping to load the barrels on."

"Just like him. He'll let anyone talk him into doing their work and never say 'boo.' And I wish you'd remember not to say 'Pa.' We were always taught to call my father 'Father.' Pa sounds undignified. Tell me, where was his fine friend and helper, Mr. Tinker? Sitting and watching?"

Aunt Addie disliked Addison Tinker. As much as Pa liked him, Aunt Addie disliked him. It made her mad that the two of them shared the same nickname. Most everyone else called him Addie but she always flinched when she heard it. She always said Mr. Tinker and made Minnie do the same. She couldn't budge her brother-in-law on that point, and he went right on being close friends with his helper and calling him by his first name. One of Aunt Addie's complaints about St. Joseph was that most of the inhabitants were far too informal. She preferred the manners of Philadelphia.

"Tend to the chickens now, Minnie, and fork some hay down for the cow as soon as you change your clothes. And hurry, you've dawdled long enough. As soon as you've finished I have some more things for you to do. Hustle now, don't be all day changing."

Upstairs in her pretty blue and white bedroom she

thought about Aunt Addie as she stripped off her school dress and carefully hung it up. She had been hanging things up carefully for so long that she didn't even think about it. She unbuttoned her school shoes and set them neatly together beside her bed, ready for the next morning. She looked at herself in the mirror as she stood there in her petticoat. A slender girl, tall for eleven, gazed solemnly back. She had fairish brown hair that wanted to curl, but couldn't because Aunt Addie wanted Minnie's hair to be as smooth and neat as her own. Minnie looked a lot like her father — he was tall and skinny and had light brown hair. Both had blue, blue eyes, very different from Aunt Addie's snapping brown ones. Minnie looked at the small painting of her mother that hung over her bed. What would her mother, if she were still alive, think about her daughter? Would she be pleased, or would she be finding fault as Aunt Addie always did? Pa said her mother had been different, even though she looked like Aunt Addie in many ways. She, too, was small and brown haired and lively, but it was a gentle kind of liveliness. Minnie tried to feel properly grief-stricken about her mother's death, but she really couldn't. Her mother had died when Minnie was born. Minnie had no memories to cling to as Pa did.

She looked at the pretty smiling face in the painting and sighed. Aunt Addie was the only mother she had ever known. She couldn't mourn for a mother

she couldn't remember, only feel sad that Letitia
Hunter Weldon had died so young, before she had
been married quite a year.

"Minnie!" Aunt Addie was calling, so Minnie
stopped thinking about her mother and hurried. She
pulled her blue calico everyday dress over her head,
mussing her hair as she did, and stepped into her
old shoes. She buttoned them swiftly, tied on a
clean starched pinafore and raced down the steps.

"Goodness, child, don't run so in the house!
You'll shake all the pictures loose! Now tend to your

outside chores — put on a shawl! It's not summer yet!"

Minnie did as she was told. It was easier than arguing. That was the only way she and her father managed with Aunt Addie. They listened to only a fraction of her steady stream of commands and suggestions, and turned off their minds to the rest. It worked, but it wasn't always easy.

She thought enviously of Annamary Goodman and the seven Goodman brothers and sisters. If only she had someone else to share Aunt Addie with, it would be so much better. Her aunt would be so busy with a big family that she wouldn't have time to concentrate all her attention on Minnie and her father. Pa said Miss Addie needed to boss the five Hunter sisters and brothers that she had left behind in Philadelphia. But they were all grown and married and had flocks of children of their own. As Aunt Addie never failed to remind them, she was needed most of all in St. Joseph, when her dear little youngest sister Letitia died in childbirth.

She had taken the widower Pierce Weldon and infant daughter Minnie under her efficient wing, and had been there in St. Joseph ever since.

It had been a long eleven years, thought Minnie. A long, long eleven years.

2

AUNT ADDIE let out a little shriek and set down her teacup with a crash. The tea slopped over into the saucer, but she didn't notice.

"Pierce Weldon, you've taken leave of your senses!"

Minnie said instantly, "Then I'm going too!"

"You are not! Neither of you is going west to find gold! And don't talk with your mouth full, Minnie. If this is more of your teasing, Pierce, I find it in very poor taste. Forget all this nonsense and finish your supper. There's gingerbread for dessert." Aunt Addie's voice was back to normal, matter-of-fact and businesslike.

"Miss Addie, I'm saying it one more time, and it's not teasing. I mean it. By sunup tomorrow I'll be out of St. Joe and on my way west to the gold fields. The wagon is loaded and my bag is packed."

Minnie repeated, "I'm going, too, Pa. I'm going along."

Her father looked at her across the table. "Minnie, lovey, not this time. This is a trip for a man.

14

You stay here all nice and cozy with your Aunt Addie and your friends and hold St. Joseph together until I get back in a little while with bags of gold, rich as Lucifer."

"It won't be a little while. It takes weeks and months to get to California, and not everybody makes it, either. There are wolves and Indians and — "

"I'll be safe enough. I've got it all planned. I'll drive hard and catch up to that last wagon train that pulled out of here day before yesterday."

Aunt Addie shoved back her chair and stood up.

"I've heard all the balderdash I can take," she declared. "Not another word out of either of you about it. If the wagon is loaded, you'll have to unload it, Pierce; and Minnie, you hush too. Neither of you is going to go traipsing off to any gold fields. You are both crazy as loons and you should be ashamed of yourselves. Help me clear the table, Minnie."

Aunt Addie went off to the kitchen with a stack of dishes. They could hear her clattering away angrily as she cut the gingerbread out of the pan. Minnie knew she had to talk fast.

"Pa, you can't leave me here. I'm going to go wherever you go. We've got to stick together. You said we always would."

"I wish I could take you, sprat, but I can't, not this time. It's a rough trip, no place for a little girl, and I'll be back before you know it."

"There've been girls and women going through here

15

all spring, a few of them, anyway, and most of them not so handy with horses as I am. And I can fish and even shoot. If you've got to go, Pa, I'd be a help, not a hindrance."

"Not this time, Minnie."

She changed her tack. "What do you need gold for, anyway? We've got enough to get along on. All this time you've been saying the smart ones were the ones who stayed home and supplied the miners. You said a man with a good livery stable could do fine selling horses to the goldminers — "

Pa shook his head. "I — I can't go into it now. Just say all of a sudden I got the gold fever. And I've got to leave tomorrow or I won't make it through the mountains before snow. The wagons that left day before yesterday were the last; anything later than that will run the risk of not making it at all."

"But why — "

Aunt Addie came in again and thumped down a plate of gingerbread squares.

"I said no more talk of going west, and I meant it, Pierce. You're only upsetting Minnie and me. Eat your supper and stop your nonsense. Take two; you're looking peaked with all this thinking you've been doing." Pouring heavy cream on his gingerbread, she said, "Now that's settled and we can forget it."

"It's settled all right, Miss Addie, but not the way you think. Tomorrow morning at sunup I'll be across the Missouri and on my way. That's what's settled."

Pa didn't usually defy Aunt Addie. He didn't obey her, either, but he didn't come right out and defy her. He just found another way of doing what he'd intended to do all along, and let her think she'd won out. There were an awful lot of things Aunt Addie didn't suspect — long days of fishing on the river bank while Aunt Addie thought he was at the stable and Minnie was at school. Luckily she was a good student and kept up with her class and the schoolteacher never mentioned it. There were hot days when Pa taught Minnie to swim, afternoons of target shooting in the woods after school.

Minnie would be scolded for dawdling at the livery stable, no place for a lady, what was her father thinking of, anyway, things'd be different if her dear little mother had only lived. Aunt Addie went on and on, but it all rolled off Minnie. She listened to the scolding and said, "Yes ma'am," "No ma'am," at the right time. All the while she was thinking of the fish jumping and the blue sky and the shade under the cottonwoods.

Father explained away the basket of fish: "Friends of mine caught more than they could use," he said, and Aunt Addie sniffed. "Fine friends, I'll warrant. They should be working for a living instead of fishing. But they are beauties, those fish. They'll fry nicely for supper."

Pa always explained later to Minnie, "Honesty's the best policy, sprat, and I wouldn't want to set a bad example. Yes, honesty's the best policy, but with a woman like Miss Addie, it's not the only policy.

17

It'd be lectures day and night if I came right out and told her we're the friends who caught the fish. Life wouldn't be worth living. But I believe in honesty, I really do, and I'd be honest with her if I dared. If she were a man, now, I could punch her one in the nose and that'd settle the argument. But she's your mother's sister, and we owe her so much, and she's a lady besides. I can't punch her and I can't argue with her."

This time Pa was arguing. Minnie began to catch on that he was serious, in dead earnest. He wasn't just talking or stringing Aunt Addie along. He was serious.

"That was your wagon you were loading, wasn't it, Pa?"

"Yes. I traded the big dray wagon for a good roomy farm wagon — there was a fellow who changed his mind about going west — and I caulked it so it'll float like a boat when I have to ford a river. I put a cover on it like a Pennsylvania wagon, and I've got that pair of big mules everybody's been trying to buy."

"I wondered why you wouldn't sell. You were offered plenty for them."

"I didn't know myself exactly. I've been playing with this idea all winter; but inside of me, I guess my mind was made up long ago and getting ready to move out. I've packed that wagon with every important thing I'll need. Now, don't you worry about me, either of you. I'll be fine."

Minnie put down her spoon. All of a sudden she

couldn't eat another bite. The lump in her throat was was as big as a lump of gingerbread.

"Then if you've made up your mind and you won't take me along, I — I guess I'll say good-bye right now. I don't want to watch you drive away."

She went around the table and gave her father a hug that almost strangled him. "Take care of yourself, Pa," she whispered. "Watch out for rattlers and bandits — "

She hurried out of the dining room before he could see that she was crying. If he didn't want her along, she wouldn't snivel and beg. And she wouldn't stand on the front step in the dawn and bravely wave good-bye, either.

"Minnie, you haven't finished your gingerbread — " Aunt Addie called after her, but she didn't turn. She didn't dare, or she'd bawl like a calf. She went up the stairs as fast as she could and made it to the safety of her bedroom before she really broke down. Then the floodgates opened and she cried. Buckets of tears dampened her pillow but she smothered her sobs. Eleven years old was too old for crying, she told herself, but she couldn't stop.

She heard Aunt Addie tap at the door. "Minnie? Minnie, child." She didn't answer. She had turned the key and although her aunt rattled the doorknob, she couldn't get in. Her voice was less bossy than usual. She sounded really concerned.

"Minnie, I've brought you some dessert. Open up, child. I'm sure your father will change his mind before morning. Minnie? Minnie?"

Finally Aunt Addie gave up and went away. Minnie had cried herself to sleep. She woke sometime later when she heard another light tapping at the door. This time it was her father. She didn't really want to talk, but she got up and let him in. In the dark he couldn't see her tear-swollen eyes, but he knew from the sound of her voice that she had been crying. He gathered her up in his arms and sat down in the rocker.

"Minnie, Minnie, how can I make you understand that this is something I've just *got* to do? I don't want to, but I can't figure any other way. And I can't explain it all to you, you're too young to understand. Just believe that I've got to go, and that I love you very, very much. I can't take you with me; it wouldn't be fair to you, but I'll be thinking of you all the time, and wondering how you are managing. Just believe that I've got to go. It won't be long until I'm back."

He rocked and rocked until finally her tense body relaxed. "We'll say good-bye now if you really want it that way. You don't have to get up and wave good-bye in the morning. I'll understand," he whispered. She whispered back, "Good-bye, Pa. I'll see you again soon. Take care of yourself."

He set her down gently and said, "Now get into bed and go to sleep again, lovey. Dawn will come mighty early." He tiptoed out, closing the door softly behind him.

The cool breeze blowing in through the open window chilled her and she shivered. Without bothering to undress, she crawled under the covers and tried to go to sleep again. She was slept out, and though she tossed and turned, sleep would not come again. Finally she got up and leaned out the window. It was late, very late. Not a house showed a light, but a thin little crescent moon was climbing the sky. It was a long time until sunup. Pa wouldn't be leaving for a while yet. If only she could go, too. She loved her Aunt Addie, sort of, and understood that under her bossy manner, Aunt Addie was a good kind loving woman. But mighty hard to live with, especially without Pa to be a buffer between them, to tease Aunt Addie out of her righteous angers, to coax Minnie to smile and put up with some of the things that drove her to distraction.

She'd have to go away, too, Minnie decided, without really meaning it. After all, if she couldn't go with her father, where could she go? Home was the comfortable house in St. Joseph; home was her own dear little blue and white bedroom with the starched white curtains and the Rob Peter quilt Aunt Addie had made for her years ago. Home was Lulubelle, the doll she had outgrown and still loved. Home was the rocking chair where Aunt Addie had rocked and sung when Minnie had an earache, and that time when the wasps on the grapes had stung her so. Home was the picture of the mother she couldn't remember, but Aunt Addie never forgot. How could she go, and where?

It was then that the idea came to her. At once she knew she would do it, no question about it. She'd

21

write a letter to Aunt Addie explaining why she *had* to go, and she'd stow away in Pa's wagon. She'd stay hidden until he had gone much too far to turn back and then he'd have to take her the rest of the way. It all seemed so easy and logical. Why hadn't she thought of it before? She had wasted her time bellering and bawling when she should have been making plans.

She shoved the little rag rug up against the door so no strip of light would shine out into the hall, in case Aunt Addie or Pa woke up to check on her. Then she lit the lamp and set to work at the table she used for her schoolwork. First the list of what she would need. Food and water for at least two days. Anything less than that might give Pa a chance to turn around and bring her back, and still catch up to that last group of wagons by driving the mules hard. No milk; it would turn to butter in the jiggling wagon. But Pa'd be glad for a pat of butter. A small covered pail of milk, then, and a big one of water. You could go for a long time without food, Minnie knew, but not without water.

If she was to be ready she'd have to move quickly. She packed her clothes — thank heaven Aunt Addie hadn't gotten around to putting away all their winter clothes. She would need warm things as well as cool. They would cross plains that simmered in the sun, and go over mountains that were snowcapped all summer.

She bundled all the things she would need in a warm blanket. For a moment she looked at Lulu-

22

belle and hesitated. No, the space Lulu would take up could be used more wisely. She jammed another pair of warm winter drawers into the bundle and sat down at her desk to write.

DEAR AUNT ADDIE,
I know you will be sorry to read this, and mad, too. I have gone off with Father to the West. Don't be mad at him, he doesn't know I'm hiding in his wagon. We'll be fine. You know I can cook, and I'll take care that we both eat well. It won't be long before we're back again. Will you please tell Annamary I said good-bye? I'll bring you a chunk of gold —

The letter was taking too long, and there was still a lot to do, so she ended it abruptly,

"I really do love you."
YOUR NIECE, MINNIE

She propped the letter up on her pillow where Aunt Addie would see it in the morning. There was the chance that Pa might come in the morning to say good-bye, even though she had said she didn't want him to. Then her whole plan would be ruined. She paused for a moment to worry, and then decided worrying was a waste of her precious time. She blew out the lamp, took up her bundle and opened the door.

The house was absolutely still, and the door squeaked a little. It seemed as if Pa and Aunt Addie would surely hear it, even though the doors to both bedrooms were shut.

The stairs creaked, but Minnie had long ago figured how to get down them as silently as possible. Keep to the left for the first three steps, then over to the right for five more, then — she must have counted wrong, for one step complained loudly. She froze. There was not a sound from upstairs. Now she was glad she hadn't been able to finish her dessert. If Aunt Addie came down she could pretend she was hunting for something to eat.

All the leftover gingerbread went into a big napkin, a half loaf of bread, a slab of cheese. She would have liked some apples, but they were down in the cellar and there was no time. The small pail of milk was easy, and so was the big covered bucket for water. It was not a lot, but it was all she dared take. It would be hard enough to get out with this much without making a sound. The napkin of food went into the big bundle, and she picked up the two pails cautiously, careful not to let them clank together.

She tiptoed down the dark hall and out the front door. Once down the walk and out the gate, she breathed easier. It was dark, but she knew every step of the way to the livery stable. She tried to run a little, and found that it wasn't practical with her bundle and pails. She settled for a fast walk, which covered the distance quickly. The darkened houses would have been scary if she hadn't been too busy struggling with her load to notice. She hurried on, past the house where Annamary was sleeping, past the courthouse, the bank, the general store. And soon, there was her father's stable.

It was locked, but she knew where the key hung. She moved a box over and stood on it. With a stretch she was able to reach the key. The lock turned quietly, but it didn't matter, there was no one around to hear. The horses and mules in their stalls whinnied sleepily. "Sshh," she whispered. "It's only me, Minnie."

She could sense the big bulk of the wagon looming up in front of her. She felt around for the wagon tongue and cracked her shins on it. "That's one way to find it," she muttered. She felt along the side of the wagon until she came to the back step, and climbed in. She couldn't see, but she could feel that Pa had it pretty solidly packed. Where could she hide that he wouldn't find her? She fumbled around until she came to a barrel. Probably flour. He wouldn't be using that right away, she was sure. Aunt Addie would pack him food for several days, at least. She'd complain long and loud at his foolishness, but she wouldn't let him go off without a huge basket of food. So the flour barrel would be undisturbed for quite a while. There was a small space behind it, not enough for comfort, but it would be only for a short time. When it was light she could get settled better. This would do for now.

She opened her bundle, stuffed the various pieces of clothing in behind the barrel, squeezed in with her pails and her napkin of food handy. She made as comfortable a nest as she could under the blanket and settled down to wait.

At the last minute she remembered her rifle. She kept it in the stable so Aunt Addie wouldn't know Pa had given it to her. She fumbled her way out again, took down her gun. While she was at it she found her fishing pole, and got back into her nest again.

Now at last she was ready to go.

3

SHE WAS STARTLED into wakefulness at the sound of her father's voice. "What the — " he said. "I could have sworn I locked this door. Damn Addie Tinker if he's going to be that careless!"

She knew for sure then that Pa had no idea she was there. He never, never swore in the presence of a lady, young or old, and he forbid swearing by others around the stable, too.

The heavy doors scraped open wider and she could hear Pa's boots on the wooden floor. The horses knew him and rose to their feet, whinnying for attention. "Hey, Lass, morning. Paddy — yes, I know you're there, Wagtail. I'll miss you, too. Wait until Addie comes. He'll feed you later."

She could hear the stamping of hooves as Pa went to the mule stall and led the big gray mules out. She knew, just as well as if she could see, how he was backing them into place in front of the wagon, with the wagon tongue between them. She could hear the harnesses being fastened, and the tinkle of the bells on their collars.

"What's the matter, Pierce? Couldn't you sleep?"

"Morning, Addie. I want to get an early start, be over the river by sunup."

"Ferry won't start running until sunup now that the gold-rushes have dwindled off. But I figured you'd be stirring early so I came down to see you off."

"I'm glad you did. Mind you take good care of the place — quiet, Willy — grab that rein, will you, Ad? — and better start off by being more careful about locking the door. I found it wide open this morning. Can't have that."

"Wait a minute, Pierce, I wasn't the last one out yesterday. You were still here when I went home for supper."

"That's right. Guess I had so much on my mind I clean forgot about it."

"How'd Miss Addie take it? What'd she say, Pierce, raise up a storm?"

"Pretty much. I knew she wouldn't like it. Little Minnie was the one who really took it hard. Couldn't bear to see me off this morning. I plan to swing around past our place on the way out. I'll wager she'll be looking out the window to see me drive away."

"That's one wager you'll lose, Pa," thought Minnie. "Little Minnie won't be looking out of anywhere for quite a while yet."

It was stuffy under the blanket but she intended to take no chances until they were so far away from

St. Joe that her father couldn't turn back to take her home. By then he'd be grateful for her company.

Pa's good-bye to Mr. Tinker was unemotional, although she knew the two men were very fond of one another. She could imagine them shaking hands.

"Still think you've taken leave of your good sense, Pierce, but good luck, anyway."

"Take care of things and keep an eye out for Minnie. Good luck to you, too."

He climbed to the wagon seat and clucked to the mules. The heavy wagon lurched forward and rolled out of the stable. It was still dark, but from the small circle of sky she could see from behind the barrel, Minnie knew it was getting close to sunrise. She was glad she had remembered to pull shut the canvas opening when she climbed in the back. Pa would really be suspicious if he found the stable door and the wagon cover both open.

"Gee," he called and the mules turned obediently down Main Street toward the Weldon house. It was good that she padded her nest well with clothing. Otherwise she would have been banged around every time the wagon swayed.

Aunt Addie must have been waiting at the front gate. Her voice sounded choked and muffled. Could she have been crying? It didn't seem possible. Yes, she was sniffling.

"Here's enough food to last you until you catch up to the wagon train, Pierce. You won't have to worry about cooking for quite a while, and then the good Lord only knows how you'll manage."

"My land, Miss Addie, feels like you've put the cookstove in here, too." Minnie could hear him grunt as he lifted the heavy basket to the wagon seat.

"Now remember to put it inside when the sun gets warm, Pierce, or the sandwiches'll spoil, and don't forget to change your stockings often; it's not healthy to go too long in the same stockings. And don't sleep on the damp ground, you'll get rheumatism; and whatever else you do, watch out for Indians. I don't want you coming back here scalped. Don't worry about Minnie; she'll be fine. And write to us often as you can; send a letter from Fort Laramie and — "

"Don't worry, Miss Addie. I'll be back soon, loaded with gold. Take care of Minnie." He raised his voice, "Good-bye, Minnie. Be a good girl and remember I love you." He was calling up to her bedroom. He waited a moment and then said in a disappointed voice, "She's still sleeping, I guess. I'd like to wake her up and say good-bye, but I daren't wait. This ferry today will be the last for at least a week, maybe much longer, now that all the wagons have moved out. I've got to make it. Good-bye, Miss Addie." He signaled to the mules and the wagon started to roll.

"Good-bye, Pierce. I still think you're doing a foolish thing. Don't be ashamed to turn back if you come to your senses — "

She was still talking as they moved away. Her voice got fainter and finally Minnie couldn't hear her at all. Poor Aunt Addie. She had another shock in store when she finally went up to waken her niece and found the letter. She'd weather the shock. Aunt Addie was like a rock. The waves could dash against her but she would be steady and solid no matter what happened.

The bumping of the wagon was bone jolting, but even so, Minnie soon fell asleep again. The next time she wakened the mules' hooves were pounding on a wooden floor. It must be the ferry, and from the look of the sky the sun was almost up. Pa was a little behind the schedule he had set for himself. He had planned to be on the other side of the Missouri River by sunrise. She heard him climb down from the wagon and walk away to exchange a few words with the ferryman. The Missouri was too wide and deep here for poles alone, but there was an intricate system of cables that held the flat boat on course, and with six men poling away they moved swiftly across.

"You're starting late, Mister," someone said. "The last bunch went across the day before yesterday. Aren't you taking a chance?"

"I know." Pa's voice was confident. "I can make pretty good time with these mules, and I'll catch up to them in a couple of days at the most. Don't you worry, I'll be over those mountains before snow falls."

"Good luck to you. I'd go myself, but my wife won't hear tell of it. She says better a live poor husband than a dead rich one."

"I aim to be both rich and lively," Pa answered.

Minnie would have loved to look out and watch the crossing, but it was too risky. She opened the flap of the blanket slightly for more air, but was careful to be covered in case Pa should look in from the back of the wagon. She could hear his jaunty whistle some distance away. He was probably leaning on the rail, watching the water. This was a good chance for her to eat her breakfast.

She was hungry and ate heartily, and was surprised at the inroad she had made on her small supplies. Next meal she'd be a lot more careful and eat only what she absolutely needed.

The crossing didn't take long, and she soon felt the wagon start and roll down a ramp to the road. They were really on their way now! They had crossed the Missouri. The next sign of civilization would be Fort Laramie, and that was about a third of the way out. It was a big country they were crossing, and she would be glad when she could ride out in the open beside her father on the wagon seat and see all that was to be seen.

Minnie had never imagined that a day could go so slowly. At first she had been busy planning and carrying out her plan, then there was the nervous excitement of wondering if Pa might possibly hunt in the wagon for something and find her too soon. But when it was clear that he would not even have to stop to prepare his dinner she felt much safer. She could thank Aunt Addie for that. The chances were he wouldn't even have to reach in the wagon until he stopped for the night, and then only for his bedroll.

He had said he planned to sleep out except when it rained, and this certainly looked like a clear day.

She couldn't tell what time it was except by the way the sun slanted on the wagon cover. The wheels turned endlessly, round and round and round, and still the sun did not shine down from directly overhead. She dozed off and on, and in between tried to move her arms and legs as much as she could to keep them from going to sleep too. There was very little room to move, and she was careful not to knock anything over. If only she could jump out and surprise Pa now. But it was too soon.

The powerful mules kept up a swift pace and the wagon rolled easily behind them. The trail to Fort Laramie was well traveled, she knew. Pa would have no trouble following it, for parties of soldiers went back and forth to the fort often. Pa talked to the animals occasionally and it was good to hear his voice.

"You're a grand team, Sam and Willy. We're eating up the miles. We'll catch up to that last group soon, and if they're too pokey for us we'll go on ahead."

Minnie didn't think the miles were being eaten up very fast. At last Pa must have looked at the sun, for he said aloud, "Sun's straight up and it's time for dinner. Just keep on going, boys. I can eat and drive, too."

Minnie reached into her napkin. A square of gingerbread, if chewed very slowly and washed down with a drink of water would do her until supper. She chewed each bite as long as she could, but at last it was gone. She wasn't too hungry. Sitting so still, she wouldn't work up an appetite and that was a good thing. Her supply of food didn't look nearly as large as it had in the middle of the night.

She must have taken quite a long nap after that, for the sun was shining low on the other side of the wagon when she awoke. Pa was whistling softly on the wagon seat and Sam and Willy were moving right along. She was stiff and cramped but all she could do was to try to move her toes inside her shoes and open and close her fingers. How she would like to run alongside the wagon, racing to keep up, breathing deeply. That would come, she thought. She'd just have to be patient.

The sun was very low when Pa pulled the mules to a stop. "Time for your feed, fellows. I'd go on farther, but if it gets too dark, we might miss the trail." She could hear him pound in the stake for their picket lines, and then unhitch the mules. The feed bags hung outside the wagon.

"A little oats for you both, and then all the nice green grass you can eat. I'll fetch you some water."

By this time Minnie realized that she had a problem she hadn't planned for. At home, a quick run to the privy in the back yard would have taken care of it. But what was she to do here? She didn't dare risk climbing out and squatting in the grass, and she certainly couldn't wait much longer. Would she have to tell Pa and chance that he would even yet turn around and take her back to St Joe? She panicked at the idea. And then she knew how she would manage. She waited until Pa went for a second pail of water for the mules. Quickly she drank the rest of the milk in the little pail. Then she managed to rise up enough to squat over it. If Pa had looked in the wagon then he would have seen her, for she had to rise up above the top of the barrel. But luck was with her, and by the time he had made the second trip she had finished and put the lid back on the pail. She had stood all the way up and stretched as hard as she could and then scooted down into her little nest with the blanket over her head again.

She was glad that Pa talked to the mules. It was the next best thing to talking with her. She started to giggle at that thought, and stifled it quickly.

"Take it easy now, Willy, you'll get yours." She heard him rustling in the food basket. "I declare, Miss Addie, you are a good one. A whole pot of coffee, waiting to be heated! And a cup, too!"

Minnie held her breath. Were the matches inside the wagon? No, apparently not. He must have had a supply in his pocket, for in the short time it would take to gather a few handfuls of dry grass and start a fire, she could smell the delicious odor of strong coffee drifting through the wagon. She didn't really care for coffee, but tonight it smelled just heavenly. She tore a piece from her half-loaf of bread and broke off some cheese. Food never tasted better.

It was quite dark when Pa reached in and dragged

out his bedroll. "Nice clear night," he said. "Stars are out. Should be a good day tomorrow."

She heard him arrange his bedroll and grunt a little as he made himself comfortable. He must have been tired, for very soon she could hear him snoring softly. The mules were tethered not far off, for in the immense quiet of the prairie she could hear them tearing at the grass with their strong teeth.

She said her prayers to herself.

"I can't kneel down, Lord, but I'm sure You understand the fix I'm in. Bless Pa and let him catch up quick to the wagon train, and get me out of here, and bless Aunt Addie and don't let her worry too much about us. Thank you, Lord. Good night."

The next day was pure misery. She had slept well, so she wasn't sleepy, and she had already thought all the thoughts she could think. She resorted to reciting her multiplication tables over and over. Then she played her own version of "My Aunt Went to Paris." She called it "My Father Went to California," and she listed in alphabetical order everything odd and funny she could imagine. But it was a dull game with only one to play it. So then she just sat and let her mind go blank while the sun climbed up one side of the wagon, crossed over the top at noon, and slid slowly, slowly, slowly down the other side. They were headed more north than due west at first, and the sun went across at an angle.

Sometimes she roused herself to imagine what it would be like in California, but she hadn't much to go on. The gold-crazed Easterners had been pouring through St. Joseph for months, but none had come back as yet. They spoke of nuggets of gold as big as your head lying there waiting to be picked up. But no one said anything about where the miners lived or where they ate or bought supplies. It was hard to imagine with no idea at all of what it was like. The climate was supposed to be wonderful, yet everyone spoke of the mountains and the fierce snowstorms that trapped the inexperienced travelers. It was hot inside the airless wagon, and she couldn't imagine snow, no matter how hard she tried. So she just sat there like a sack of oats and felt the wheels under her jolt round and round.

By the third morning she had eaten the last of her carefully hoarded food. Pa must surely be getting close to the bottom of Aunt Addie's basket, and soon he would have to come sorting through the wagon for things to cook. Her stomach growled with hunger and her mouth felt as dry as flannel, for she had finished the water, too. And she ached all over from the jouncing. She tried to hold out as long as she could. She would say to herself, "When that front wheel squeaks one hundred more times I'll pop out and surprise Pa — if I'm still alive." But at the end of the hundred turns when she found she was still alive, she would try for a hundred more, and then just one hundred more.

They were going up a slight rise, some of the cargo shifted to the back of the wagon, and Pa was encouraging Sam and Willy. "That's my good fellows! Up the hill, boys; who knows what lies on the other side — Yippee!" he shouted, and Minnie was so startled she almost jumped right up. "Yippee! There they are, boys! There's the wagon train, no more'n an hour away!"

This was the moment, then. Pa surely wouldn't turn back when he had caught up to the last company. And there might even be a woman and some children in the group, and he'd see that it was all right for her to come along.

She stood up and stumbled to the front of the wagon, where the cover was laced tight except for a small circle in the center. She poked her head through the opening and said shakily, "Surprise!"

4

MINNIE JERKED AT THE CORD that tied the canvas wagon cover and hopped through the opening onto the wagon seat.

"Surprise, Pa!" she said again. She had been prepared for shock, for outraged anger, for a glad welcome, and she got all three in quick succession.

"Wha — wha — what — !" he stammered. "Minnie! Sprat! What are you doing here? Where did you come from?"

"From the wagon," she answered gaily. "From behind the flour barrel, and I'm mighty glad to be out in the air again."

"But what are you — "

"Going west to the gold fields with you, Pa. I couldn't let you go all that way by yourself."

He put his arm around her and gave her a great bear hug. "Minnie, Minnie! What am I to do with you? Aunt Addie, does she know?"

"She does now. I wrote her a long letter and told her not to worry; we'd be home soon with the gold."

"You'll be home sooner than that, Minnie. We're turning right around this minute and heading home."

"You can't take me home now! You won't be through the mountains before the snows if you lose even one more day. You said so yourself. That's why I waited so long before I surprised you."

"What a surprise! Oh, Minnie, why did you have to do this? Why did you spoil my only chance?" He hugged her again and put his cheek against hers. In a moment she felt a splash of tears. Pa was crying.

Minnie was frightened. Grownups scolded and bossed and raged and sometimes spanked, but they never cried.

"Pa, what's the matter? Don't, don't, please don't feel so bad. We can go on to the coast, we'll manage fine. I even brought my gun along. I can help put meat on the table, maybe. Pa, don't cry!"

He raised his head and brushed away the tears. "A grown man like me. I'm ashamed of myself," he said sheepishly. "It's just that I was so disappointed. We can't go on, Minnie. I can't take you on a trip like this. We'll go back, and it'll be all right. You just didn't understand, that's all. You didn't understand."

Minnie was bewildered. "Why is it so important, anyway? You never cared before about being rich — we were making out fine with the livery stable. You said yourself we'd never had such a year as last year. Why does the gold matter so much?"

He paused a long time and then said, "It was to buy my freedom."

"You're a free man, Pa. How could you buy your freedom?"

He thought awhile and said, "Minnie, you remember that nice little schoolteacher you had two years ago?"

"Miss Allen? Of course."

He tried to put his thoughts into words. "You know, I was mighty taken with her. She'd a suited me just fine, and you, too, I thought; and I think she liked me too. Sweet and gentle and kind — but that's as far as I dared go."

"Well, if you liked her and she liked you —"

"Honey, I've got only one house, and no house would be big enough to hold your Aunt Addie and another woman, no matter how nice and gentle and easygoing she was."

Minnie nodded. Pa went on to tell her how much they owed Aunt Addie. She had come west from Philadelphia to St. Joseph, planning to stay long enough to help with the new baby. And when the baby, who was Minnie, was born and Letitia died, Aunt Addie had stayed on.

"She never gave it a second thought; she just stayed to take care of us. She left her friends and her church works and all, and came out here to the very edge of civilization. She didn't like St. Joe that much, never has, but that didn't matter. She was needed here. She wrote back and sold the family house that had been left to her — she being the only one of the children not married. She went to the bank here and plunked down the money to pay off the mortgage on the house and the livery stable and never said a word to me until it was done. Said she wanted to be sure we always had a roof over our heads. Even most of the furniture is hers — all that nice fancy Eastern stuff. She's all the mother you've had for eleven years, lovey, and while her tongue is sharp, she's got a wonderful good heart. Remembering all that, I couldn't bring myself to think about bringing another woman home to push her out, couldn't even think about it. Then when the news of the gold rush came, I thought — why not? Why not go out and get a fortune quick, and give Miss Addie the house, lock, stock and barrel, and have enough to keep her in nice style. We'd build another for us nearby so she wouldn't miss you too much, and with any luck I'd find another lovely woman like your mother who'd be willing to marry me — " He put his head down in his hands.

"And you'd use the gold to buy your freedom! Pa, don't go back! Don't give up. We'll go out West together; you'll see, there'll be lots of other women and girls going and I'll be perfectly safe. I can be a help on the way. I can drive and cook and shoot squirrels — "

"No squirrels out here on the prairie."

"Rabbits, then, and we'll have fried rabbit. Please! You'd be buying freedom for both of us."

When Minnie first clambered out onto the wagon seat and Pa had dragged on the reins in surprise, Sam and Willy had stopped obediently. But when he sat talking for so long with no directions to them, the mules moved on. So the wagon was getting nearer to the wagon train every minute. In the clear air they could see the wagons rumbling on ahead, and every turn of their wheels took them nearer.

Every turn of the wheels also made Minnie's arguments harder to resist. By the time they caught up to the encampment, which was now stopped for supper, Pa was almost convinced. He still said he'd have to sleep on his decision before he was sure he was doing the right thing.

To Minnie's joy, this particular company of gold-seekers had a woman among them. She was a big, loud-talking person who told them that when her "old man" and her three grown sons got the gold fever, she told them they could go only if they took her along to take care of them and keep them out of bad company.

Minnie was lucky, and she knew it. Few women went to the gold fields. These gold-seekers were not settlers but men who planned to get rich quick and take their wealth back home. Here and there a family went out to hunt for gold and use the money to set themselves up on a farm in the pleasant California climate. But mostly the hopeful goldminers were a mixed lot. There were professional gamblers, and men who had never been able to make good at any job, hopeless losers in life, and impulsive men who had left jobs indoors knowing nothing about outdoor life. There were men who were wanted by the law, and others who would be as soon as word of their thievery got out.

If Pa hadn't happened on Mrs. MacNear in the first wagon he approached, he might have made up his mind the other way. But he wanted so much to go on, and so did Minnie, so he wasn't too hard to persuade. He still said he'd have to sleep on it, but when his first cooked supper was over and his first real campfire was only a few glowing coals, when Sam and Willy were crunching away at the sweet prairie grass, Minnie settled down to sleep with an easy mind.

Pa made her a comfortable bed in the wagon, took his gun from its place under the wagon seat, where it could always be kept dry, and made his bed on the ground by the wagon. His last words were, "Now, don't count on anything, Minnie. I'm still not decided. Good night, sleep well."

She didn't worry. Pa had decided, whether he knew it or not. He didn't toss or turn one bit, but fell asleep almost as soon as he lay down. A man with a real problem doesn't sleep like that, she thought. She was asleep not long after.

Just as she expected, in the morning he said he had thought it all over, and since they had come this far, and there was a woman in the group to be company for her, he and Minnie would continue on to California.

"Provided," he added, "that you write a letter to your Aunt Addie and mail it at Fort Laramie. That's maybe five hundred and fifty miles away; maybe you could write a little each day. That way Miss Addie'll know how things have been with us each

day and she won't worry. She'll scold a lot, but she won't worry so much."

Minnie started a diarylike letter to Aunt Addie with an entry each day. After the first long description of how she hid in the wagon and how they had caught up with the wagon train, there wasn't too much to say. She put in quite a lot about Mrs. MacNear from Pennsylvania, not too far away from Philadelphia. She stressed Mrs. MacNear's motherly, kindhearted qualities, and left out the loud voice. Aunt Addie wouldn't care too much for Mrs. MacNear, although she would be honest enough to admit she was a woman who meant well, even if she did bellow like a bull at her husband and sons.

"Rab!" she would holler, in a voice that carried all

along the line of wagons, "Rab! Git me a rabbit if you want fresh meat for supper, or eat salt pork all the way to Californy if you're too lazy to git up off'n your butt!"

Aunt Addie would shudder and say, "Cover your ears, Minnie. Such talk is not appropriate for a young girl to hear." So Minnie left those parts out, and only mentioned that Mrs. MacNear had made a big pot of hearty soup and shared it with them, and had taught Minnie how to bake corn bread in a skillet over the fire.

The trip itself was uneventful. Downright dull, really. They rolled on, mile after mile, under clear skies through the green prairie grass, following the wagon ruts of the travelers who had gone before them. When Minnie tired of riding she would jump down and run alongside the wagon for a while for exercise. Sometimes she rode for a while with Mrs. MacNear, who generously shared her knitting needles and wool and helped Minnie knit a scarf for her father.

Pa didn't encourage her to socialize with any of the others in the group, beyond a polite "Good Morning." Unless she was with Mrs. MacNear he kept a close eye on her.

"There's every kind of man in this bunch," he warned. "Not all of them are too upstanding by any manner of thinking. Some of 'em are downright crooks, I wouldn't wonder. I don't trust their shifty eyes. Keep your gun loaded and at hand, sprat, and don't hesitate to haul it out if any of them hangs around the wagon when I'm not here."

He was almost always there, except when he went off occasionally to hunt. "Might as well have fresh meat now, we'll need our store of dried meat for later on."

Occasionally they had a rainy day to break the monotony of endless sunny days. Pa fastened a large wooden bucket where it would catch the soft sweet rainwater for drinking and cooking, and saved the water in the big keg for the times when they did not camp near a stream or spring.

Mostly they bumped along in the bone-shaking springless wagon hour after hour. Minnie and her father had always had a lot to talk about, but even they ran out of conversation and rode for hours in silence.

Minnie liked it when they came to the Platte River. They followed along its banks, sometimes on one side, sometimes on the other, depending on which side had low flat banks where the wagons could go easily. They crisscrossed back and forth so many times that fording was no longer a novelty. At this time of year the river was wide and shallow, so the mules didn't have to swim and the water reached only part way up the wagon wheels. Pa watched the wagons ahead of him, and when he saw one of them lurch into a deeper spot, he got out and led the mules around that place. He splashed along, hardly waist deep, but told Minnie she was to stay high and dry on the wagon seat.

One day when the sun was especially hot, she

49

pretended she had slipped off the seat and jumped into the water. Pa was alarmed, but she splashed and floundered just out of his reach. The water was cool and it felt wonderful. The warm sun soon dried her off and she was not in the least harmed by the experience.

"See, Pa, I'm not frail and sickly. A little swim didn't hurt me at all."

He had to admit she was right, and after that he let her paddle around a little whenever they crossed at a shallow place. It made a change in the monotonous routine.

The trip was dull, but not at all unpleasant. The blue sky stretched endlessly above them, a breeze blew, birds rose out of the tall prairie grass singing as they flew. The wild flowers were different from those in Aunt Addie's carefully planted garden. Minnie didn't always know their names, but she delighted in their color and fragrance. In her letter to Aunt Addie she pressed a few of the blossoms, so her aunt could share them too.

The long hours on the wagon seat gave her plenty of time to think, and she did a lot of thinking about Aunt Addie. When she was away from the constant orders and complaints, she could see better how kind and good Aunt Addie really was underneath her brusque manner. She put some of this new thinking into her letter. Without saying it in so many words, she was able to express her love for Aunt Addie in the things she wrote. She only regretted that the letter would take so long to get back to St. Joseph.

Fort Laramie made a change in their routine. It marked the first long part of the journey over, the easy part. They rested there a day, fixed any worn parts of the wagons, stocked up on supplies. The Weldons did not buy much, for Pa said the prices the Fur Trading Store was charging were pure banditry. Minnie left her long letter there, to be taken back to St. Joe the next time a batch of furs or a military report was sent east.

After Fort Laramie the scenery changed. The flat prairies and rolling hills became mountains. In the mountains the trail narrowed, sometimes to a path only wide enough for one wagon, with a towering cliff on one side and a deep ravine on the other. This was a real test for drivers and animals. The sure-footed mules had no difficulty, but just to be sure, Pa walked along and led them, talking constantly and soothingly and keeping them on the right track. Minnie sat in her father's place and held the reins. She kept her eyes firmly on Pa and the mules, and didn't look at the steep drop so close by. Up ahead, horses reared and balked, and Minnie's heart was in her mouth for fear a wagon would be jerked over the edge. She didn't enjoy this part of the trip.

"I don't know why I complained that the prairie was tiresome," she said shakily once after they had maneuvered their way through an especially difficult spot. "I'd settle for a few miles of prairie right now."

"So would I," said Pa, mopping his forehead. "And so would Sam and Willy, I'll bet. But it'll be easier going for a while now, according to the scouts at Laramie. We're going to follow the Sweetwater River through this valley up ahead. It'll be easier on all of us."

The Sweetwater River flowed through a green, pleasant valley, and they all, humans and animals, had a chance to rest and relax a little. Beyond the valley, at South Pass in the Rockies, all the streams and rivers flowed westward, and the water had a disagreeable taste and terrible color. Many of the travelers were made sick from drinking the alkaline water, even though they had all been vigorously warned about it at the fort.

For the most part the gold hunters were a careless, devil-may-care lot, who paid little attention to sober warnings about the dangers ahead. They thought only of the treasure they were going to find in California, and talked incessantly about the wild spending they would do as soon as they picked up their first bag of nuggets.

Pa used the water he had stored in his wooden keg back when the Sweetwater was sweet and clear. It soon had a stale taste and was warm and unsatisfying. The July sun was boiling down now, and Minnie thought she would give anything for a cold drink of water. But at least they did not get sick, and that was something to be grateful for.

The hard pulling was beginning to tell on the mules, strong as they were. Pa rationed the water he had brought from the Sweetwater, but the animals never really had enough to drink or eat. Those with horses had even more trouble, and several wagons full of gold-seekers dropped off at Fort Bridger, frightened by the prospect of crossing the desert and of getting over the Sierras before the early snows blocked the passes. They saw wrecked wagons as they crossed the desert, and often came to a pitiful pile of bleached bones by a dry waterhole that marked the end of the trail for another would-be rich man.

Pa tried to distract Minnie's attention by laughing and joking so she wouldn't notice the bones. She saw, and knew what they were, and inside she was icy cold with fear, even though the heat was almost unbearable. She tried not to let her father know. He had enough to think about, and he was constantly haunted by the thought that he should have taken Minnie home back there when he first discovered she had stowed away.

He worried about the blazing sun, tried to fix a flap of canvas so it would make a small spot of shade over her seat, and wiped her parched face with a dampened rag to give her a little relief.

"We won't have to tell Aunt Addie about this part," she said, trying to laugh a little. "She'd be distressed that we didn't have enough water to take a bath in."

They finally made it across the desert, although at the time no one in the wagon train was sure they would. Suddenly, almost without warning, the trail started uphill, and they were out of the desert and into the foothills of the Sierras. There was fresh water again, and cool air, and spirits rose once more.

And then they got their first real glimpse of the mountains ahead. It was really frightening. Even Mrs. MacNear was subdued into talking quietly. It was late August by now and snow in the high passes could be expected any day. The nights and mornings were cold, and Pa had brought along only enough blankets to keep himself warm. Minnie had just one, so they huddled together in the wagon bed and shivered all night long.

"At least the way is well marked," Pa said. "We won't get lost if we follow the wagon tracks. And if other groups got through, so can we."

Mr. MacNear shook his head. "Home never looked so good to me," he said. "Makes me wonder what in tarnation I was thinkin' about to get all of us out here."

Mrs. MacNear refused to be discouraged. "We'll make it," she said. Minnie wondered if she really believed it, or was trying to cheer up her family.

The haul up the mountains was hard. They had been warned about it at Fort Bridger and knew what they had to do. They pooled their horses and mules, and used five or six teams to pull each wagon up the steep rocky trail. At the top they unhitched, tied a strong rope to the back axle, and took a turn with the rope around a sturdy tree. Slowly, slowly, inch by inch, the men let out the rope and eased the wagon down the western side of the hill. It was backbreaking, muscle-tearing work, and few of the men were as fit as they had been before they started across the desert.

Then another shift of tired animals would pull the next wagon up, and another group of tired men would let it down until finally all of them were over the last of the High Sierras.

Minnie and Pa had unloaded everything they could from their wagon to make it as light as possible, and Minnie made many trips back and forth before it was all loaded again. They camped there two nights, too exhausted to go on. Two good nights' sleep, fresh water, the last of the autumn grass for the animals to graze on, and the prospect of easier traveling from now on made most of the party feel like new.

Minnie made light of the hardships in her letters to Aunt Addie. There was no need to frighten her aunt and Minnie didn't like to think of what they had endured during that awful crossing of the mountains. The close calls, the times the mules had almost plunged off the trail, the bone-weariness that numbed body and mind — she didn't care to dwell on all that. And really, compared to the horrifying experiences many parties had, their group came through remarkably well. Many were sick and discouraged, and the wagons had been mended and patched over and over. Several men suffered from frostbite, most were so sick of salt pork and corn bread that they had little appetite, but not one human and only three animals had died on the way.

So Minnie stressed the breathtaking scenery and the bracing mountain air and did not mention that a few flakes of snow had started to fall as they struggled through the last pass.

5

THEY PARTED from most of the wagon train when they rolled into a lovely lush valley on the western side of the mountains. There were a few farm-houses and barns, but the land had been overrun with hundreds of goldminers working their small claims. Many of the men they had come out with did not want to venture any farther, but Pa decided to go on to San Francisco and then find a place where the ground had not been so thoroughly worked over.

They left the MacNears there. It was hard to say good-bye to a family they had traveled with for so many weeks and had come to know so well. They exchanged home addresses and hoped they would meet again sometime, but all of them knew it was not very likely.

"It's a peculiar feeling," Minnie said to her father, "not knowing where we'll be living or what we'll be doing, or if we'll ever meet the MacNears again. In St. Joe we always knew we'd see our friends the very next day, or next Sunday in church at the latest."

He agreed that it gave him a strange rootless feeling, too. "It won't be for long, sprat. We'll be back in St. Joe before you know it."

They continued down the pleasant Sacramento valley, and not long after that Minnie could write, "A wonderful sight, Aunt Addie! The harbor is beautiful, and crowded with ships from everywhere in the world. I saw flags of more nations than I knew existed. Everywhere you turn, you hear different languages spoken. It is amazing."

She didn't add that it was far from civilized. "There are Chinese here, and Mexicans and strangely dressed people from the Sandwich Islands, and Australians and Peruvians and Swedes, and of course, our own Easterners. I will watch everything and it will be very educational." That would please Aunt Addie, she thought, and reassure her.

She did not mention that the beautiful harbor was crowded with ships abandoned at the dock or swinging idly at anchor farther out. Passengers and crew and finally the captains had abandoned ships in the wild rush to the gold fields. Later, ships' captains learned to anchor well out and allow the passengers to get off as best they could in boats rowed out by local small boys. The crews were kept on board at gun point, and as soon as the ship was unloaded and reprovisioned, the captain headed out to sea again. Even then, sailors sometimes jumped overboard and swam ashore, so eager were they to try their luck in the gold fields.

Minnie learned a lot of this later. Now she only

knew that it seemed strange to see the fine ships abandoned and uncared for. And stranger still to see the flimsy shanties that had been built all along the waterfront street. Odd pieces of lumber and canvas and colorful pieces of calico formed walls and roofs of stores and houses. It looked as if a strong push would knock any of them down, yet this was where people lived and did business.

The Weldons drove along the waterfront street and looked in amazement at the motley crowds that swarmed all around them. It was like nothing they had ever seen before.

There were men of every color and costume, and some with hardly any costume at all, just a flowered cloth wrapped around them like a skirt. Others wore tailcoats and tall silk hats and might have been going to a formal party. There were wagons and carriages and ox carts; there were men on horseback and muleback and on burros and hundreds more walking and running. There was no pattern to the traffic. It surged one way and then the other. Whips cracked, horses reared and plunged, men yelled and swore in many languages. Clouds of dust swirled up from the unpaved street and settled grittily on hair and face and teeth.

Finally Pa said, "Enough of this. Let's find a decent place where you can stay — a place where there's a good woman to look out for you, and I'll get on my way to the fields."

"Can't I go along?" she wailed.

"Nope, not if I can find a proper place for you to

stay while I'm gone. I'll have enough to answer for, without explaining to Miss Addie that I took you to a mining camp.

"I haven't seen one woman yet in all this mob."

"Well, I've spotted several," answered Pa rather grimly, "and none of them looked like a good influence on a young girl."

He asked people from time to time and got either a blank stare and a shrug, or "No spik Ingleesh." Finally he asked a man who came out on the steps of a cabin marked "The Emporium."

The man scratched his head and said, "Well, yes, there's Mrs. Stanhope. She lives up on the top of that hill," pointing to his right. "But watch your step as you go up. She comes out with a gun, ready to shoot any rascal she thinks has his eye on her two daughters or their chickens. Yell ahead that you mean no harm and have the little girl stand up and wave. Otherwise she just might put a bullet through the crown of your hat."

It sounded pretty wild to Minnie. She thought briefly of what Aunt Addie would think of all this. Then she put that thought out of her mind. This was a different world entirely. Aunt Addie's standards did not apply at all.

"Can't we leave the wagon and walk up? Sam and Willy are tired."

"And let some crook make off with everything we've got? No siree, not on your life. We'll manage."

They toiled up the rutted road, passing a group of

shacks and tents that were thrown together even more flimsily than those on the main street.

Sam and Willy pulled willingly and soon the steep hill leveled off into a good-sized field fenced off for grazing. A brown horse looked over the fence at them. The small house and barn looked substantial, as if they had been there for some time. They halted at the gate. Just as they had been warned, a woman came out on the porch with a rifle.

"Don't come any closer," she yelled. "Stay right there and state your business!"

"We don't mean any harm, ma'am," Pa yelled back. "Stand up and wave, Minnie," he added and then yelled again, "I'm looking for a safe place for my daughter to stay for a while. I was told you have two daughters of your own and might be willing to take a third. Drat it," he said to Minnie, "I can't carry on a conversation at the top of my voice with a gun pointing at me."

Fortunately Mrs. Stanhope decided that he looked honest. "Drive in and leave your rig. It'll be safe enough if you lock the gate."

Once they were on the porch Mrs. Stanhope was very cordial. "Sorry about the gun, Mister — "

"Weldon, ma'am, Pierce Weldon from St. Joseph, Missouri, and this is my daughter Minnie."

"I'm Hannah Stanhope. Come in Mr. Weldon. You look clean and you've got good manners, even if you haven't much sense. Whatever made you bring a young girl out into this madhouse? Come inside and set awhile. Ruby," she called, "put the

61

kettle on for tea and you and Pearl come here to meet some visitors. Now, what were you thinking of to drag a youngster out here? It's no place for decent people, let me tell you!"

"I didn't exactly bring her," Pa explained. "She stowed away in my wagon and I never knew it until we were pretty well along."

"So? Well, she's got spunk, and she'll need it to survive out here."

Mrs. Stanhope was a little woman. She hardly came to Pa's shoulder. Her gun was almost as tall as she was, and though she put it down, she never left it far from her hand. She was weathered and wrinkled as if she had worked hard outdoors most of her life, and she was almost as brown as the men on the street below, the ones Pa said must be from the Sandwich Islands.

Two pretty girls came shyly out from behind a flowered curtain. "Ruby and Pearl," said Mrs. Stanhope. "My daughters, mine and my husband's, and I'm here to protect them with my life if need be. And you can guess from that mixed bunch you saw down below that I might have to."

"Have you lived here long, Mrs. Stanhope?"

"Mercy, no! And won't stay here a minute longer than we have to. We've a good farm — or we did have — over in the valley along the Sacramento. We were among the first to come out here, long before gold was ever thought of. I wish those days were back," she added. "We lived like civilized people then and could ask a traveler in without threatening him first. But those days are gone, until this craziness wears itself out and they all leave. Our farm was near Sutter's Mill, and overnight we were overrun with the trash of the world, squatting right in our own yard and staking out claims everywhere. Never a by-your-leave or please, just moved in wherever they thought they'd strike it rich. Trampled the crops, scared off the cows, stole the horses except for the one out there. Finally we couldn't stand it anymore, and we came here to stay with my cousin Charlie. We found his house empty, most of the furniture stolen, but the house and the barn were still standing, at any rate. Charlie must have left for the gold fields. Josephus — he's my husband and you might call him St. Joseph if you wanted, a better man never lived — he decided that since we'd lost almost everything and would have to start all over again, he might as well get rich off the gold, too. So he's in Rich Bar, and as soon as he has a poke of gold we'll buy some land and make a new start somewhere else."

There was very little furniture in the house, only three chairs and a table and two beds. Mrs. Stanhope offered her visitors a chair and sat in the third herself. Ruby and Pearl served the tea and then stood shyly to one side.

"Sounds like a good plan," commented Mr. Weldon, sipping his tea.

"Meanwhile, Rich Bar is no place for well brought up girls, so we're staying put here."

This gave Pa the chance to say, "Sounds very wise of you, ma'am. And that brings me to my problem:

where to leave Minnie where she'll be safe with good people until I have my poke of gold. I don't want any harm to come to her."

"Hmmm, we're good people, right enough, and I'm doing my best to make it safe, but it's not easy to scratch out a living here. We brought our pen of chickens, and our cow, and we just barely manage by selling eggs. The eggs they bring down from Oregon sell for two dollars, but by the time they get here, they're pretty gamey. So for fresh eggs I can get two-fifty each and the hens are laying fine."

"Two-fifty *each?*"

"Wait until you see what the other food costs, and a bed for the night without even clean sheets — and a hot bath! I could make a fortune if I'd turn this place into a hotel, but I won't, not for the class of folks as would come here. No siree, I won't! Not with my two girls to protect: I guess if Minnie's a nice dispositioned child and willing to help around it wouldn't be any more trouble to protect a third. It's the least I can do for another mother."

"Her mother's gone, ma'am. My wife passed away when Minnie was born."

Mrs. Stanhope rose and enveloped Minnie in a hug that left her breathless. Little as she was, Mrs. Stanhope had a rib-cracking hug.

"Poor motherless lamb!" she exclaimed. "Then of course I'll take her and keep her safe until you come back. Unpack your things, Minnie, and my girls'll show you where to hang them."

"I haven't much, ma'am, coming off so unexpected."

"You won't need much fancy out here, I can tell you. The scum of the earth is gathered down below and we don't socialize with them. You're to obey without question, Minnie, do you understand? If I say come in, you come running and hide in the closet with Ruby and Pearl. You understand? Same as my own child."

Minnie nodded. It had all happened so fast. One minute she was riding along with Pa, and the next minute she was to be the child of a strange woman in a strange house halfway around the world from Aunt

Addie and St. Joe. Her head was whirling. Still, it was an adventure, and that was partly what she had come for. It was just that she had expected a different kind of adventure.

Pa was pleased, she could tell. There was no doubt of Hannah Stanhope's sincerity or of her determination. And Minnie knew already that San Francisco was no place for a little girl alone.

Mrs. Stanhope said Mr. Weldon might as well rest himself and the mules for a night, before taking off for the gold fields. In the meantime she'd tell him all she knew about the various mining camps.

"They change so fast. One day the place'll be nothing at all, and then word gets out of a strike and they come swarming in by the hundreds. Then when that stream bed gives out, off they go to another place to build another bunch of tumbledown shanties. So you don't know from month to month. Last word I had, my Josephus was in Rich Bar, but he might have moved on."

"You get word of him, then?"

"Oh, yes, it's not much of a problem if you remember to send the same message back with three or four miners. That way, at least one'll stay sober long enough to leave the letter off at the Emporium before he goes off to get drunk and squander all the gold he's found. I ask every day when I go down to sell the eggs."

Pa was relieved. "Then you'll be hearing from me often, sprat, and you be sure to write your Aunt

Addie. There must be some ship going back that'll carry mail."

They had a good, though very plain, supper and soon after went to bed. Ruby and Pearl shared one bed and Mrs. Stanhope made room for Minnie. Pa spread out his bedroll in the hayloft and in the morning he said it made a wonderful change from sleeping on the ground.

"You'll get a bellyful of that," warned Mrs. Stanhope. "Remember in the mining camps, you keep your gun beside you all the time, and never get out of sight of your mules and wagon. Things'll get stolen as soon as you turn your back. Good luck and a full poke soon. Don't worry about Minnie. She'll be fine."

Tears welled up in Minnie's eyes as Pa waved goodbye and rolled out the gate. She did not cry, though. Tears had no place in the new tough life she was about to lead in this faraway town. She'd miss Pa, but even so she looked forward eagerly to the next step in this extraordinary journey. At any rate, it would not be dull.

6

HANNAH STANHOPE gave Minnie no time to feel lonesome or left behind. "Let's be about our business," she said briskly as soon as the wagon was out of sight. "Do you know anything about chickens, Minnie, you being a city girl and all?"

Minnie explained that St. Joseph was not really a city, only a small town, and that her Aunt Addie kept chickens, too. "I always had charge of the chickens," she said. "They were my chore."

"Good!" Mrs. Stanhope was pleased. "Come along, then, and we'll gather the eggs and hope they've done well by us this morning. I want to trade for a fish for our supper. The fishermen have all gone off to the diggings so it's up to the old men and the little boys to keep a supply coming. There's fish being shipped down from up north in Oregon, but it's just dreadful expensive and none too fresh. The hotel men have driven the price way up beyond belief, for they can serve even old fish to the mob here and they'll pay through the nose for it."

Talking all the time, she led Minnie out to the chicken coop. "We used to let them run, but we found out that bunch in the shacks and tents down below were helping themselves to a chicken dinner whenever they wanted one. Good laying hens! So we got brush and brambles and made a fence that discourages the thieves some — that and my gun. The chicken house is padlocked every night, too — I'll show you where I hide the key."

There were eight lovely eggs in the straw nests. "That's twenty whole dollars!" marveled Minnie.

"Wait until you see how little twenty dollars will buy," said Mrs. Stanhope. "They tell me flour has gone up to *four hundred dollars* a barrel! Fortunately we've still got quite a bit left, but I use it sparingly, I tell you. Now we'll get ready and go down into town to sell these. We all go. I'd rather leave Ruby and Pearl up here, but they can't flourish a gun the way I do. I couldn't hit the broad side of a barn door, but I've let it be known that I'm a crack shot, and my reputation as a gunfighter has spread, you know. Now don't ever mention that to a soul, promise."

Minnie promised and added that she was a pretty good shot, that her father had taught her.

"Pity you didn't bring a gun along."

"Oh, but I did. I brought my squirrel gun all the way from St. Joe, and ammunition, too. It's in your closet."

"Well, now! I hope you'll never need it, but it's a comfort to know you can handle it. I don't even own a bullet for mine, but nobody knows that it's all bluff and hot air, and it helps a lot. You'll see what I mean. Now let's get ready and go into town."

Ruby and Pearl had washed the breakfast dishes and swept out the house and were ready. They were beautiful girls, fair and pink and white, with eyes as blue as Aunt Addie's best china. Ruby was seventeen, taller than Pearl, with heavy honey-coloured hair, and Pearl was sixteen with hair as yellow as wheat. They were shy and soft-spoken, and indeed, did not talk much at all. Their mother did enough talking for all of them.

They put on large sunbonnets that covered their hair completely and shielded their delicate complexions from the warm sun. More important, the bonnets hid a lot of their pretty faces. It was hard to hide the fact that they were graceful and slender and well formed, but Mrs. Stanhope had done her best. They wore rather baggy cotton dresses, and shawls that were very concealing. It was too warm for woolen shawls, but Mrs. Stanhope was firm.

"Put this one on, too, Minnie, and don't complain, any of you," she said. "I'll not have you pinched and fondled as you push through the crowds. Minnie, you wear a bonnet, too."

Minnie had not thought to pack a sunbonnet on that busy night so long ago, and would rather have done without it, but Mrs. Stanhope insisted on supplying one of her own. It acted like blinders on a horse. She couldn't see out of the sides, only straight ahead. She wanted to be able to see everything, not to miss a thing.

Mrs. Stanhope carried her gun on her shoulder; Ruby carried the basket with the eight precious eggs, and they started off down the hill. Farther down, the road wound through the higglety-pigglety cluster of tents and shacks that she and Pa had seen the day before. From the door of almost every dwelling a man or two appeared, to whistle or call out to them as they passed.

"Eyes straight ahead, girls. Don't pay 'em a bit of mind." Mrs. Stanhope swung the gun from her shoulder and held it in two hands, ready to aim. The whistling stopped suddenly, and just as suddenly all the men disappeared inside. Minnie smothered a giggle. If only they knew the gun wasn't loaded, and that Mrs. Stanhope couldn't fire it if it had been.

"But she'd lay about her with the butt end," thought Minnie. "There'd be many a bruised head if anyone tried to come too close."

"We never lived like this before," said Mrs. Stanhope sadly. "A stranger passed our farmhouse, we'd invite him in to set and eat, and most likely he'd stay a week before movin' on. My Josephus is a wonderful hosty man, he loves visitors. Well, nothing's been the same since this gold fever hit everybody, but someday we'll have a farm again away from all this, and we'll be able to walk down the road and speak courteously to our neighbors."

They hurried down the main street by the water-

71

front, ignoring the passersby who called out to them or reached out to try to touch them. The dust was inches thick but Mrs. Stanhope instructed, "Let your skirts drag, girls. Don't lift 'em an inch. Better be dusty than call attention to your ankles."

Minnie didn't have to worry. Her skirt was above her shoe tops, but her only pair of shoes would soon be ruined. She would go barefoot, she decided, if Mrs. Stanhope would let her.

The crowd they were pushing through was fascinating. Here were three men with slanting eyes — Chinese, she decided, but she was disappointed that their skin was not the bright lemon yellow she had expected. They wore long pigtails down their backs and cone-shaped straw hats. She had no time to stare, for here came a group of half-naked brown men in skirts of patterned cloth. "Look the other way," hissed Mrs. Stanhope, and the three girls obediently turned their heads. Then there were Mexicans with flat black hats, brilliant waistcoats covered with embroidery and long fringed sashes. And everywhere, everywhere, mobs of dirty, ragged, unshaven men pushing and shoving.

When they finally made their way to the Emporium, the storekeeper looked up and greeted them. It was the same man who had directed the Weldons to Mrs. Stanhope's house only yesterday. Only yesterday? It didn't seem possible that so little time had passed.

"Well, I see you've got another chick under your wing, Mrs. Stanhope," he said. "I've got two letters for you, here."

She ripped them open eagerly and read the few lines rapidly, then sighed with relief. "He's fine as of last week and getting a sizable amount of gold," she said. "The diggings are so good in Rich Bar he won't be back for a while. And this one — this letter was written much earlier — "

The storekeeper laughed. "The first feller came straight here and left it before he headed for the saloon. The other didn't make it until he'd sobered up after his binge, and by that time the news was pretty old."

"And he was flat broke, I'll wager."

"Flatter'n flat. Had to head right back to Rich Bar to make up his losses. Now what have you for me today?"

"Eight eggs, new laid."

Before the storekeeper could answer, a well-dressed customer said eagerly, "New laid eggs! I'd give my life for a fresh egg; haven't had one since I left New York four months ago! I'll take four at fifty cents each!"

The storekeeper snorted. "You sure are newly arrived, Mister. I have to pay two-fifty and they're all spoken for already."

"Two-fifty *each?*" The man gasped, and then said gamely, "I'll make it three, ma'am."

"Three-fifty, Mrs. Stanhope, and that's all," said the storekeeper. "Tomorrow they'll have to go back to two-fifty, of course."

Before Mrs. Stanhope could agree a clear voice from behind them said, "Four-fifty would be fairer, for he's selling them for five each." They all turned to look at the speaker. She was well dressed, or had been before her black silk dress had gone through a long sea voyage. It was stained now with salt water, and wrinkled, but she wore it with style. Her bonnet was tied under a firm little chin and black curls escaped from around the edge. She was surrounded by luggage.

"Is that so?" Mrs. Stanhope asked the storekeeper. "Haywood, have you been underpaying me, and me so trusting?"

He nodded sheepishly and tried to explain. "Everyone's getting all they can get, why shouldn't I? I was planning to raise your rate, anyway." He turned to the young lady, "That wasn't very fair of you, Miss, just when I was about to suggest that maybe Mrs. Stanhope would make room for you, too. I was going to do you a big favor, for it's the only place in town that's fit for a lady. Now you can go to Emma's, for all I care. I hope you can sing and dance."

"I'll handle this, Mr. Haywood. No respectable girl is going to be started on the downward path at Emma's Dance Hall, not if I can help it. You are respectable, Miss?"

"I'm Daisy Palmer from Boston, Massachusetts, and I'm very respectable, ma'am, and planning to stay that way. I came around the Horn on the *Adelaide*, landed just today."

"*Alone?*"

"I started off with my father, but poor father fell

74

ill a month out from Boston and died. So now I'm alone. I was planning to teach school here — we were told in the East that San Francisco had schools and churches — "

Mrs. Stanhope groaned. "You poor child, the lies they've printed about this town, and here it is, a collection of tents and shanties and bad men and a few bad women. Not much work for a teacher, and you all alone in the world, too! You're welcome to live with us. It's safe and clean and proper, but I don't know how far our rations will stretch. The hens'll slow down their layin' soon, and that's our only cash crop except for a few vegetables."

Miss Palmer turned to the storekeeper who was listening to all this with interest. "Mr. Haywood, since I've been waiting here you've had at least four requests for hardtack, and you say you're all out. If you've got flour and some sort of a stove I could turn out a pile of hardtack everyday. At the prices you are charging you could afford to pay me a small wage."

The stranger who had bid on the eggs joined in. It was all absolutely fascinating, thought Minnie, the way everybody minded everyone else's business. Like something in a book. No one stayed a stranger long.

"There you are, Haywood, and no excuse for being out of hardtack. Take the young lady up on it, quick, or I'll offer her a job and set up in business next door to you."

The storekeeper thought a moment. "I do need a steady supply — all right, it's a deal." He was going

76

to set the wages, but Miss Palmer said firmly, "We'll talk money when I see how fast I can work and how much you'll be able to get for the hardtack."

"You've got a good head on you, Miss," Mr. Haywood admitted reluctantly. "All right, start tomorrow morning. I've a stove in my back room and a place for you to work."

Mrs. Stanhope said, "Then pay me my eight times four-fifty — "

"Thirty-six dollars," calculated Miss Palmer quickly.

"Thirty-six dollars," repeated Mrs. Stanhope. Mr. Haywood groaned, and then took the money out of his cash drawer. He took the eight eggs carefully out of the basket and shook his head.

"Out-bargained, and by a woman, too."

They each picked up a piece or two of Miss Palmer's luggage and started home. The bags were heavy.

"What have you got in here, Miss Palmer? Stones?"

"Books, mostly. I was going to start a small school of my own as soon as my father found enough gold to buy us a house and land." She sighed. "There goes one dream, I guess. I've always wanted a school of my own, and I'll get it, too, someday. But not nearly so soon as I thought. And please call me Daisy. If I'm to live with you we might as well be friendly."

The introductions were made all around as they trudged up the hill, past the tents again. Mrs.

Stanhope unslung her gun and aimed it at the tent colony, and no one said a word to them.

"Got 'em trained now. The trouble is, this bunch'll move out as soon as they get their supplies, and a new crowd'll come in. And the training is to be done all over again. They ought to save themselves some trouble and put a sign up. 'Beware of Old Woman With Gun!' Most of 'em couldn't read anyway, so I'll just have to keep totin' this thing."

7

———

DAISY PALMER started work early the next morning.
The sun wasn't quite up yet when she was stirring
around, starting breakfast for them all, and walking on tiptoe so that the others could sleep a little
longer. Inspired by her example, Minnie slipped
into her clothes and went out to feed the chickens
and gather the eggs.

The air was cool and fresh, and the sky westward
over the bay was glorious with colors reflected from
the rising sun in the east. From high up on the hill
she could see everywhere, the hundreds of masts
sticking up in the harbor, down the roads to the tent
village, the roofs of houses that clung to the hillside
and overlooked the street along the waterfront.
From up here it looked peaceful and clean and good.

She wondered about her father, and how he was
doing. She missed him, but she was not disappointed
that he had left her behind. Life in San Francisco
promised to be as adventurous as anything she would

find in a mining camp, and she liked the Stanhopes and Daisy Palmer.

The rooster crowed at the rising sun, and she hurried back to the house. The rooster would rouse Mrs. Stanhope, and the day's activities, whatever they might be, would begin.

She was right. Mrs. Stanhope and Ruby and Pearl were awake and dressing modestly behind the curtained doorway of the closet. Daisy was making pancakes. They smelled delicious.

"You could have added an egg," said Mrs. Stanhope. "Look, Minnie's got nine today, and we made a real profit yesterday. We can spare one to eat."

"Let's wait and not be extravagant," said Daisy. "They won't lay like this forever. In the meantime we can be thinking of some other honest way to earn a little money. From my observations yesterday I gather there are plenty of dishonest ways."

"You're right, Daisy," answered Pearl. "The miners come in from the gold fields dying for a bath and a clean shirt and some entertainment, and the gamblers and the saloon keepers and the dance hall girls are waiting to take whatever gold they've found. They don't care if they do it honestly or not."

"Thank heavens for good men like my Josephus and your pa, Minnie. Whatever gold they get, they'll hang on to and not squander it on drink and cards and fancy women. But men like that are few and far between out here. Most of 'em'll come here broke and go home broke and nothing to show for all their backbreaking work."

Daisy left soon after breakfast to go down to the Emporium. "No, there's no need to go down with me. I can manage fine — no one will insult *me*. I'll see you all later when you come down to bring the eggs, and I'll let you know how I'm doing. I've never made hardtack before, never saw any until we were on the ship, but the ship's cook told me how it was made."

"I'll feel better if my gun and I go with you as far as the tents. Let's go now, before the men in the tents are up. They sleep late. We'll come down to escort you home tonight."

While Mrs. Stanhope was gone they began the morning chores. They made up the beds, washed the few dishes and swept out the one-room house. They milked the cow and set the pail in the shade. The horse was grazing contentedly.

Mrs. Stanhope said, "Lucky the grass lasts a long time in this climate. I don't know what we'll feed him when it's gone. There are no oats to be bought in town, and if there was, it'd cost a fortune. There's plenty out there on some of those ships in the harbor, making a banquet for rats. What a waste!"

They cultivated the small vegetable garden and Mrs. Stanhope said how grateful she was that they had collected seeds before the ruffians overran their farm. It was the seed from last year's trampled crops that made even their little garden possible. And she was determined to let enough of this year's garden go to seed to supply them when they had land again and a place to plant.

"I don't care if Josephus doesn't get *rich* rich, just enough to get out of here and make a proper home again. I'll never get over what they did to our nice place in the valley. Almost breaks my heart whenever I think of it." She hoed vigorously as if each weed were a goldminer that she was routing out.

After that it was time to take the nine eggs to the store. "Nine times four-fifty; quick, girls, figure it out so Haywood can't cheat me. I'll never sell him an egg so cheap again."

The store was crowded and they had to wait outside until a few miners bought their supplies and left before they could squeeze in. Mrs. Stanhope held the basket over her head so no one would bump her and break her precious eggs.

"Six dollars!" shouted one tall man who could see in the basket. "Six dollars apiece! I haven't had a fresh egg for weeks!"

"No sir," said Mrs. Stanhope firmly. "I'll do my dealing with Mr. Haywood, and you can buy from him. I treat him honest and he treats me honest." She had pushed up to the counter by then, and Mr. Haywood winced as she said this. She grinned and said, "That'll be four-fifty apiece, and after that you're welcome to charge any price you please."

Mr. Haywood would rather the deal had been made in private where he could argue, but he had no choice. He reached into his cash box and paid the money, but not gladly.

"Anyway," he said, "your new boarder has brought me luck. She's a fast worker. I've sold a pile of hardtack and promised more as soon as she can get it baked. You go on back, she's busy back there. Need any supplies? I got a shipment of salt and it's going fast."

Mrs. Stanhope shook her head. "Only a fool or a millionaire would buy salt from you. We'll go back to see Daisy."

Daisy was busy indeed. She was glad to see them and said so, but never stopped working a minute. Her bakery in the lean-to shed was makeshift, a flat door on two barrels for a mixing table, and a pot-bellied stove to bake on. The stovepipe went out through a hole chopped in the wooden wall. The roaring fire had heated the stove almost red hot, and from time to time she dashed a pail of water on the wall around the stovepipe whenever she noticed the wood was starting to smolder.

"I scrubbed the stove lid as clean as I could and I'm baking directly on it. It's not the way I'd bake at home, but then nothing's the way I'd do it at home."

Mrs. Stanhope agreed. "We're on our way down the beach past town where the water's clean," she said. "We're going to boil a couple of pails of sea water down for salt. You won't catch me bargaining my life away for salt when there's a whole bay out there free for the taking. Do you want to come with me, Minnie, or stay and give Daisy a hand?"

Minnie really wanted to go. It was a chance to explore a little and see more of her strange new surroundings. But she could see that Daisy needed a helper, someone to feed the fire and throw water on the wall while she mixed and rolled and baked. So she elected to stay.

"I'll go with you to the beach another day," she said.

"Oh, there'll be lots of times to go. Two pails of water makes only a little crust of salt, you know. We have to go every couple of days."

They went on while Minnie stayed to help. Daisy dumped a pile of flour in a mound on her table, made a hole in the center where she poured in salt and water, and mixed the whole mess with her hands until it formed a smooth firm ball. She floured another section of the table, rolled the ball out in a thin sheet using an empty bottle, cut it in six inch squares, pricked it all over with a bent fork, placed as many as possible on the hot stove lid, turned them over after a couple of minutes, and laid the finished products on a shelf to cool. Mr. Haywood came in from time to time to gather up all she had made.

"Quick," she said to Minnie, "go out and see what he's charging, so I'll know what he's got to pay me. Don't let him see you."

That was easy. She stayed close behind a broad man and Mr. Haywood never noticed her at all. "Fresh Hardtack!" he was shouting. "Made right on the premises by a gentle refined woman's hand! No weevils, no dirt, pure and fit to eat! Will keep for weeks! Two dollars each, and a bargain at that!"

Minnie gasped. Only flour and water and salt at two dollars each! Mr. Haywood had no trouble selling them at that outrageous price. The miners bought all he had and clamored for more. She hurried back to the lean-to with the news.

"Good work," said Daisy. "I've made a pile of them already this morning, and there's still plenty of flour in the barrel." She did some quick mental arithmetic and was ready for Mr. Haywood the next time he came back for more.

"Time to talk about salary," she said cheerfully.

"Haven't time, the store is full!"

"They'll wait. I want fifty cents per piece."

"Fifty cents! I'll go broke at that rate!"

"Then pay me whatever you think you owe me for the morning and I'll stop right now." She started to wipe her floury hands on her apron.

"No, wait," he said. "Don't be hasty. Let me think about it and figure a little — "

"I've already saved you that trouble." She untied her apron and folded it into a neat bundle.

"That last batch'll burn!" he yelled. "Wait, don't go! I'll pay it! I'll pay it! Fifty cents apiece, my word on it."

"I'll keep track of the number with charcoal on the wall here," she said, "although you may tally, too, if you think I might not be accurate. And I want my pay at the end of each day. Agreed?"

"You've got me over a barrel," he groaned. "I agree."

She put on her apron again. "Don't worry, you'll make a fortune on this, and we won't do badly either. Minnie is my new helper. I'll pay her out of my

fifty cents, so don't go having a fainting fit, now. I could insist that *you* pay her, you know."

He groaned again, gathered up the pile of fresh hardtack and hurried out. Minnie stood there open mouthed.

"You will help me, won't you, Minnie? You'll earn fifteen cents apiece and I'll keep thirty-five cents and together we can make a nice profit. And the miners'll pay gladly for bread that's at least clean and not wormy. Put some more wood on the fire, and fling some water, will you? That'll be your part, to keep one fire going and the other out."

Minnie grabbed several sticks of wood and jammed them into the stove, and then threw the rest of the pail of water on the smoldering wall. She worked hard that day, harder and faster than she had ever worked before. She chopped and carried wood and brought pails of water from the well behind the store. Daisy worked fast, and now that she had help, she was able to turn out hardtack in an uninterrupted flow. She tallied the number on the wall with a piece of charred stick.

When evening came and the store was closed, they banked the fire, collected their pay and stumbled out to where Mrs. Stanhope and her daughters were waiting to escort them home.

"Now we can pay for our room and board," said Daisy.

"I couldn't take your hard-earned money," protested Mrs. Stanhope. "You're both welcome to share what we've got."

"Please take it and don't argue," said Daisy Palmer. "Winter's bound to come, even in this climate. When the garden and the chickens slacken off, you'll be glad of the money."

Mrs. Stanhope finally agreed. Minnie was beginning to see that Miss Daisy Palmer was a determined young lady who generally accomplished what she set out to do.

"If you like, I can be thinking of a money-making plan for you, too," she said. "Something you and the girls can do up here at home, perhaps. There must be some service you could perform."

"No baths," said Mrs. Stanhope. "The miners'll pay anything for a hot bath, but I don't want them coming up here and wanting their backs scrubbed. Anything else, yes, but no hotel and no baths."

"It'll be something else," Daisy promised. "Don't worry about that. Now that supper and the dishes are done, I'm for bed. I'm worn out."

"Go right on to bed," urged Mrs. Stanhope. "You two must be tired. I'll wash out your apron and by morning it'll be dry. I'll do your work dress, too, Minnie. That's the least I can do to help. Tomorrow you must take an apron, too, Minnie. Ruby and Pearl, how about a little music before we all turn in?"

Ruby went to the closet and brought out a fiddle case. She handled it as tenderly as if it were a baby. "Her pa's fiddle, he taught her to play." When the fiddle was in tune, she and Pearl began to sing in harmony. It was the prettiest music Minnie had ever heard. Nicer, even, than the church choir in St. Joe on Sunday. They played and sang hymns and the songs that everyone was singing like "Oh, Susannah," and then sweet love songs. Minnie went to sleep to the tune of "Mavourneen," and slept soundly until the rooster crowed to mark the start of another day.

8

AND SO BEGAN a period of the hardest work Minnie had ever done in all her eleven years. Her hands were calloused and rough from carrying wood, and her arm muscles grew strong from all the chopping and water carrying. She went up the hill each night exhausted, and came down in the morning refreshed from a good night's sleep to do it all over again. Every day Daisy collected their pay and gave Minnie her share, and every day the pile of coins in the pottery jug grew bigger. Sometimes they were paid in gold dust on the days when Mr. Haywood had taken in more gold than coins.

One day when she showed up at the Emporium, Mr. Haywood said, "A letter came for you, Minnie. I'll bet it's from your pa." She riffled through the pile of messages, some so dirty and crumpled it was hard to tell who they were intended for. When she found hers, she tore it open eagerly.

"I usually make a five dollar charge for holding mail," Mr. Haywood remarked. "Can't afford to run a post office for nothing, you know, but for a friend I'll forget it."

Daisy grabbed up the heap of letters, separated them into alphabetical piles and jammed them into the lettered pigeon-holed cabinet hanging on the wall. It all happened so fast that Mr. Haywood stood there openmouthed.

"I usually make a twenty-five dollar charge for sorting mail," she said, "but for a friend I sort free. Looks like we're twenty dollars ahead of you, Mr. Haywood, and what's more, any more remarks like that and I'll charge you."

Mr. Haywood shook his head in amazement. "I never knew a woman who could get the better of me in a deal," he said. "I'll never enter into a trade with you."

"It's no special talent," she said pertly. "All you have to do is be smarter than the one you're trading with. What's the news from the gold fields, Minnie?"

"Pa says he's well, but not finding much gold where he is, so he's moving on to Hangtown. That sounds like an awful place."

"One's no worse'n another," said Mr. Haywood, "nor better, as far as accommodations are concerned. Thirty men in bunks in one room, bugs in the straw mattresses and all for two dollars a night. They throw the smell in free."

"Pa has his own wagon to sleep in, thanks be. He won't have to sleep jammed in with a lot of others. Maybe at Hangtown he'll find a pile of gold."

"Some do, some don't, said Mr. Haywood. "I still say a man can make more staying behind than he can out there working his legs off to find gold."

"A man can do it, and a woman can, too, if she keeps her wits about her."

"No doubt about that," said Mr. Haywood admiringly. "You never forget to keep your wits about you do you, Miss Palmer?"

"I try not to," Daisy answered. "A woman alone has to figure out some way of taking care of herself. Come, Minnie, let's get started on our work."

It was a relief to know that her father was safe and well. She would be glad to see him, and proud to tell him how well she was managing. She had not even touched the small sum of money he had left to help pay for her room and board. She thought of the jug partly filled with coins already. She and Pa could buy their freedom together.

It was that very day that the idea came for some respectable gainful employment for the Stanhopes. The flour barrel was getting low and Daisy sent Minnie into the store to remind Mr. Haywood that they would soon need some more. He was talking to a customer and Minnie waited politely, but impatiently, for them to finish. She didn't want to be away too long from her stove and stovepipe. The customer, a well-dressed man in a frock coat, was saying, "Not one shirt? It doesn't have to be fancy, Haywood, any clean shirt will do. This is so soiled it'll never come white again. I've never in my life worn a shirt two days in a row before I came out here, and I've worn this one for three weeks. The boats from the Islands won't wait even long enough to take on a load of laundry, and the Sandwich Islanders don't iron them, either. The China ships take weeks to get sheets back. What we need in this town is a laundress."

"Things here don't work the same as they did back East. Here, you get a laundress who could do even plain washing and ironing, and she'd be off to Emma's place, dancing and drinking with the customers. Make more there in an evening than she would in a month of washing and ironing."

An idea flashed into Minnie's mind. As the stranger turned to go, she tugged at his coattail. "I can get it washed for you, sir," she said. "Washed and ironed and back here by tomorrow. How much would you be willing to pay?"

The man turned and looked at her in surprise. "Haywood, what's a little girl doing running around in this town? It isn't safe."

"She's safe enough," said Mr. Haywood. "She's got two of the fiercest watch dogs I ever saw guarding her."

"I don't need a watch dog," said Minnie proudly. "I'm a good shot myself, and nobody'll meddle with me. What about it, sir? Do you want your shirt washed?"

"Do I?" He grabbed her up, lifted her right off the floor, kissed her cheek, and set her down again. "You are an angel from heaven! I'll pay ten — no, twelve dollars, and a bargain at that."

"Ten will be enough," she said. "We aren't hoggish. And make it around noon tomorrow. If the fog comes in at night, things don't always dry so quick on the line."

"Where do you live, little girl? I've a pile of shirts in my room and I'll gladly take them to your place."

"No need," said Minnie firmly. "Pick up and delivery will be here at the Emporium around noon. If you want the rest washed today bring them right away."

She gave Mr. Haywood the message about the flour and hurried back to the lean-to. The wood around the stovepipe had started to smolder and she flung a pail of water on it before she took time to tell Daisy about the shirts.

"I hope it'll be satisfactory to Mrs. Stanhope," she worried. "I guess I should have asked her first before I offered, and set the price and all. But it's a respectable job and the customers never have to go near the house. There won't be any miners or gamblers or anybody coming up to upset Mrs. Stanhope."

Daisy thought it was a fine idea, and the price was fair, considering how much everything else in San Francisco cost.

Mr. Haywood came back for a moment to say admiringly, "You two really have a nose for business. I never thought of running a laundry. That man was Dan Lawrence, runs a gambling house, The Red Rooster. He and his fancy friends'll have a wagon load of laundry every week, and they can afford it, too. Course I'll have to make a charge for allowing my store to be used — say, half — five dollars a shirt."

"Oh, no," said Daisy. "Fifty cents a shirt is more than plenty. It's pure profit for you, and folks'll come into the store and buy groceries, besides. It's pure profit for you. Fifty cents, and the rest goes to the Stanhopes."

He shook his head. "Aren't you and Minnie going to keep some of the ten for yourself?"

Daisy explained frostily that one did not make a profit on friends, "Not when they took both of us in off the street and shared all they had. No, nine-fifty per shirt is all theirs. We'll work out a price list for other pieces tonight and post a sign here tomorrow."

So The Elite Laundry was started. While the Stanhopes were washing, Daisy discussed prices and wrote out a neat list to be posted in the store. "Shirts —three dollars, pillow cases — two dollars. Undergarments — five dollars each, whether or not they require ironing. The ladies in Emma's place will be interested, I'm sure," said Daisy.

"Ladies!" snorted Mrs. Stanhope. "Ladies! There's not a lady among them."

"Women, then. They're bound to like the idea of sending their laundry out, if they are as prosperous as Mr. Haywood says."

The next day around noon the three Stanhopes came down the hill as usual, only this time instead of just their basket of eggs and the lunch pails for Daisy and Minnie, they carried a pile of clean white shirts, starched and pressed to perfection. More laundry

was waiting for them, a pile of petticoats from Emma's place.

"I told them ten dollars each for the petticoats," said Mr. Haywood, "seeing as how they're all so frilly and ruffly. Seemed fair."

"You're right," said Daisy, crossing out the five and raising it to ten on her list. "They can afford it, too. As I hear it, the miners come into town and carouse all night and when they sober up, they find they've left their whole poke of gold with Dan Lawrence's gamblers or Emma's girls. Those miners are certainly a foolish bunch."

"Not my Josephus," said Mrs. Stanhope.

"Not my father," said Minnie.

And so a new routine was established. Now all five were working very hard, but it was not unpleasant work. They allowed themselves an egg apiece a day, and did not even try to sell the vegetables still growing in the garden. They planned to store what they could for later on, and they ate all the fresh vegetables they wanted. They yearned for an occasional treat of meat, and once in a while Mrs. Stanhope bought a slab of dried beef at the Emporium. Shaved thin, creamed and eaten with homemade sourdough bread it was delicious. Bacon was available, too, but at an outrageous price, and Mrs. Stanhope indignantly refused to pay it.

"We'll have our own farm soon, and we'll butcher our own hogs. In the meantime, we'll manage and save our hard-earned money."

Everywhere around they saw examples of waste and extravagance. Tools were scarce, and miners who had not had the forethought to bring along their own cheerfully paid a hundred dollars for a pickaxe and even more for a basin to wash their gold in. They didn't mind, for they all expected to be enormously rich in a very few days. Some were, but most of those were so overcome with their riches that they drank and gambled it all away. Others had their pokes stolen before they even got back to town. Pokes and tools and donkeys and food supplies, everything stolen.

Pa wrote that he made his camp as far away as possible from the rest of the crowd at Hangtown, and never let Willy and Sam out of his sight for a moment. He had not found the huge nuggets that rumors said were everywhere, but steady panning everyday was producing a fair amount of small nuggets and flakes. The money changers who set up business in the camps to buy gold were real frauds, he felt. He wanted to hang on to his gold until he could trade it for money without being cheated. So it might be safer if he brought it back to Minnie in San Francisco. He was lonesome for her anyway, and wanted to make sure she was all right.

The days were so full that they flew by. Minnie lost track of the time. It seemed as if she had been in San Francisco forever, putting fuel on the fire and fetching water.

They all slept soundly. There was no oil available for the lamp, so there was no reason to sit up late at night. They went to bed at dusk with the chickens, and got up with the rooster's crow at dawn.

It was hard, but there was a satisfaction for all of them in working toward a goal. If they grumbled, and they all did occasionally, it was only because they were tired and cross and homesick for the different kind of life that they had led before.

"Sometimes I think I never want to see another piece of hardtack," said Daisy. "Sometimes I wish I had never suggested the idea to Mr. Haywood, and then I wonder what I'd be doing if I hadn't. One of these days I'll have my little school, and this will all seem worthwhile."

"We need a change," said Mrs. Stanhope. "Give us a tune, Ruby, love, something sweet and pretty to get our minds off baking and washing and ironing."

When Ruby began to play, "For I'm going to Californy with my basin on my knee," Mrs. Stanhope snorted.

"They can keep their basins on their knees, most of them, for all I care. I still say, nothing but trouble has come from all this gold madness. I'm glad my Josephus doesn't have it. He'd never have left the farm if he hadn't been driven off."

Still, the tune was lively and cheerful, and they all went to bed feeling better because of it.

9

IT WAS NOT OFTEN that Ruby had the time or the strength to play her fiddle at the end of a long day, but the girls sang as they washed and ironed. Mrs. Stanhope made all of them rub her own homemade mixture of mutton tallow and camphor into their hands. She had brought a precious crock of it with her when they left their farm. It smelled terrible but it did the job of healing and soothing their hardworking hands. None of them really minded the hard work — it was like a strange span of time between the life they had left and a much better life for all of them in the time to come.

One night they were awakened by the sound of sobbing. It was Daisy, crying in her sleep, in the bed that she shared with Ruby and Pearl. They shook her gently to waken her, and wiped away the tears that were running down her cheeks.

"I — I was dreaming about my father," she said dazedly. "He was alive yet, and laughing the way he used to do. Oh, I miss him so!"

Mrs. Stanhope soothed her. "There, there, dearie. It's too bad, too bad, but the Lord's ways are not always clear to us. You have to think of him in a better place where there's no more sorrow or misery."

"He was sickly even before we started," said Daisy. "He never was really strong since my mother died years ago. He thought the sea journey would be good for him, and the milder climate out here — and instead of that — " she began to cry again. Mrs. Stanhope fixed her a cup of warm milk and Ruby got out her fiddle and played softly in the dark. She and Pearl sang all the hymns they knew, and Minnie hummed along. Soon the warm milk and the music did their work and Daisy Palmer fell asleep again.

Minnie had thought of Daisy as crisp and bright and self-sufficient. This was a new side of her, frail and sad, and as much in need of comfort as the rest of them. By the next day Daisy had recovered and was in control of her feelings as usual. But Minnie remembered and thought, "That's a face she puts on for the public. Inside she's as mushy and lonesome as I am."

It was a good face, though, an ideal face to show to a town where each person had to be constantly vigilant. Daisy, in her starched pink gingham work dress with her stiff white apron over her arm, and Minnie by her side carrying her squirrel gun, walked through the crowded waterfront street as if the motley mixtures of people did not exist. They attracted plenty of attention, of course, in a town where almost no respectable women were to be seen, and not many of the other kind, either. Daisy ignored the remarks and invitations and dodged around those who put out a hand to stop her. She seemed not to hear the cursing and swearing that went on everywhere, and she came out of it completely untouched and unruffled. Even with her gun, Minnie was not anxious to go out on the street alone, but when she was with Daisy, she was not at all afraid. She was glad, now, for the sunbonnet that hid most of her face. She could hurry along and not meet the eye of any of the passersby. It was easier that way.

Daisy was more than a match for Mr. Haywood and his conniving, and seemed to enjoy their clashes. She collected their pay every day, and double-checked the laundry bills to make sure the Stanhopes got what was due them for their hard work.

It was a strange existence, far removed from what Minnie had known back home in St. Joseph, Missouri. Their routine was unvarying, except on Sunday when they all rested. But it was not dull, not when ships from all over the world were arriving daily. There was always something new to see.

One morning she and Daisy arrived at the Emporium extra early. A big bearded seaman in a fine braid-decorated uniform was waiting there, with a young boy at his side. The man tipped his hat politely and wished them good morning. Daisy and Minnie responded with polite nods. They had learned not to encourage conversation with strangers, no matter how nice they seemed. After a while the silence grew strained. It was awkward to just stand there waiting on the steps of the store in silence. Daisy finally looked up at the early morning sky and remarked that it looked as if it was going to be a pleasant day. The man answered eagerly that it did, indeed, and then introduced himself and his young companion. Minnie had been eyeing the boy from under the brim of her sunbonnet, and wishing she could talk to him. He seemed to be about her age, and it had been a long time since she had talked with anyone her age — since she left St. Joe, actually.

"Captain Thomas Cavendish, ma'am, of the ship *Mary Elizabeth* from Boston, and my ward and cabin boy, Thomas Dowell. I should say formerly of the *Mary Elizabeth*, for all my crew has left me stranded. They got away in the night and are already headed for the gold fields with most of my cargo of tools. The rest of the cargo is there at the dock, and I've no one to unload it."

"That is a predicament," said Daisy. "What will you do?"

"Go off to the gold fields myself, I guess. I might as well pan gold until this gold fever is over. Then I'll gather a crew again and sail the *Mary Liz* back to Boston. I wish I could dispose of some of that cargo, though. I don't want it to lie there and rot, or be eaten by rats. I'd sell it for whatever I could get."

Daisy was holding Minnie's hand, and Minnie felt a squeeze. As politely distant as before, Daisy asked, "And what does your cargo consist of, Captain Cavendish, sir?"

"Flour and sugar mainly. The men made off with the tools."

"How much would you charge for the flour and sugar?"

"I'm told it's bringing a pretty penny out here, but that's unloaded and delivered. It's not worth a penny in the hold of the ship."

"If I made you an offer, and got it unloaded myself — "

"Whatever I could get, ma'am. Forty dollars a barrel would be welcome. It'd be forty dollars more than nothing, which is what I've got now."

"Sold!" Daisy said briskly. "I'll buy the lot, sugar and flour, and promise to make payment by this time tomorrow. Is that agreed? My hand on it."

She offered her hand and he shook it wonderingly.

"I've never in my life made a deal with a woman," he said. "I hope you know what you're doing. I'd hate to think I was taking advantage of a helpless lady, Mrs. — "

"Miss. Miss Daisy Palmer, lately of Boston, now of San Francisco."

"From Boston, too! Well, this is a small world, though it seems large enough when you're out at sea. I do thank you, Miss Palmer, and — "

"Miss Minnie Weldon of St. Joseph, Missouri."

Thomas and Minnie smiled shyly.

"Thomas is as stranded as I am, Miss Palmer, and wants to go to the gold fields with me. His late mother and father were my good friends and I'd hate mightily to have him come to harm in what I hear are mighty rough mining camps. Yet I can't leave him here to shift for himself."

Daisy was silent for a moment, thinking. Then she said, "I could take care of Thomas, if you like, and give him employment in helping me with my work. He would have good meals in a respectable house, and payment for his services. I can vouch for his safety if he promises to obey me."

Captain Cavendish said eagerly, "Thomas is a good boy, a little rambunctious sometimes, but a good boy, really. Thomas, you'll stay here with Miss Palmer. It won't be for long. When I get a crew together we'll sail back in the *Mary Liz.*"

"But I want to go with your, sir!"

"This is an order from your captain, Tom. You know a seaman never questions his captain's orders."

"Please, before you decide, you must inquire about my references, Captain Cavendish. You know nothing of my character."

"Ma'am, I haven't been a sea captain for twenty year without becoming something of a judge of character. I think I can trust you. I know a fine woman when I see one. Tom will be safe with you."

She blushed at the compliment, but still she insisted, "Nevertheless you should inquire, Captain Cavendish. It is only right. Mr. Haywood, owner of the Emporium, can vouch for me. And at noon the rest of our household will be here. I hope you will plan to meet them before you make up your mind."

"If you think so, Miss Palmer, but somehow I don't think it is necessary."

Mr. Haywood arrived then, hurrying to unlock the front door for his first customer of the day. Daisy and Minnie went back to the lean-to to start the fire and begin work.

"Daisy, do you have enough money to buy the whole cargo, even at a bargain of forty dollars? That could be an awful heap of money."

"I don't, but Mr. Haywood does, I'm sure. I'll sell it to him for fifty dollars a barrel, and he'll be getting such a tremendous bargain that he'll find some sobered-up, flat-broke miners to unload it in return for a grubstake to start back to the fields. See if he doesn't jump at the chance. He'll grumble, but he'll jump."

Daisy was right. Mr. Haywood jumped for joy at the chance to get a whole load of sugar and flour at fifty dollars a barrel, and Daisy made a ten dollar profit on each barrel without even taking off her sunbonnet. The captain was delighted, for he had thought the cargo would be a total loss, so there was satisfaction all around.

At noon, the Stanhopes came down the hill to the Emporium with the laundry. The captain was charmed with the two pretty shy girls, so soft-spoken and well brought up, and pleased with their peppery little mother. He could see that they were scrubbed within an inch of their lives, and their aprons were spotless and starched. He nodded approval when

Mrs. Stanhope said firmly, "We're fussy about cleanliness, Thomas; we think it's next to godliness, and godliness is very important, too. There'll be no sailor language allowed under our roof, mind. But we'll try to make your stay pleasant, and I'll fatten you up a mite for the trip home. Daisy, here, might give you your lessons. Minnie's been neglecting her studies out here, and that's not good."

Thomas was reluctant about the whole thing, and still wanted very much to go to the gold fields with Captain Cavendish, but his seaman's habit of obedience to his captain held, and he did not argue at all.

The promise of a comfortable bed in the hayloft, and three good meals a day after four months of rough sailing weather sounded welcome to the boy. Perhaps the idea of a little motherly fussing appealed to him too. So another orphan was added to the Stanhope household, another stray taken in.

10

M INNIE HAD BEEN with adults only for so long she had almost forgotten how nice it was to have someone her own age to talk with, someone with whom she could share jokes, someone to giggle with. Thomas Dowell fitted right into the household as if he had always been there. He had been shifted around considerably in the past two years, living with different relatives after the death of both his parents. His father had been lost at sea and his mother had gotten a fever and died shortly after. Finally, when he was almost twelve, his godfather, Captain Cavendish, took young Tom to sea with him as a cabin boy.

"I would have been a sailor, anyway," he told them. "My father, Cap'n Dowell, sailed out of Salem. He was a good captain, everybody in Salem said he was one of the best. He never had trouble getting a crew. They lined up for a chance to serve under him. I want to be a captain, too, someday. I will, I know; I'll make it somehow."

"Of course you will, if that's what you want, lovey. But for now, it's enough to look out to sea and watch the ships come in. You'll be back on that dangerous water soon enough."

Mrs. Stanhope shuddered. The idea of a sea voyage did not appeal to her. "I'm a landsman," she said. "I'm a farmer through and through. The closest I want to get to sea water is to dip up a pail for salt. Which reminds me, maybe that can be one of your chores, Tom, now that the girls and I are so busy doing laundry. We're running low."

Tom agreed eagerly. "I had just got properly toughened up when we landed here," he said. "I just got used to the hard work so I didn't ache all over every morning when I got up. I want to work hard so my muscles won't get soft and flabby. Captain Cavendish says maybe I can be a midshipman when I'm only fourteen if I've got the strength for it."

Daisy chuckled. "Don't worry about your muscles getting flabby, Tom. We've enough work here to keep your muscles strong and to develop some ones you didn't know you had."

It was arranged that Tom would carry enough water in the morning to take care of all the laundry needs. Then he would go down to the Emporium and help chop wood and carry water for Daisy and Minnie. He could bring the freshly washed clothes down, and take back the day's collection of dirty clothes. And for this he would be paid a wage out of the laundry and baking profits. He was pleased with the arrangement and so were they, and so it was decided.

He was a good workman, fast and cheerful. He whistled and sang sea chanties and laughed when his changing voice skidded upward an octave. "I'd better stick to whistling. I can count on my whistle." He kept as clean as Mrs. Stanhope required, and enjoyed baths in fresh water after long months of sluicing off in a bucket of sea water. He kept his shock of brown hair combed as neatly as he could, but no one scolded much if he got rumpled and dirty at his work. When they did, he teased and wheedled and laughed until everyone was happy again.

Every Sunday after the necessary chores of milking and straightening were done, they sang a few hymns and Daisy read from the Bible. There was no church in San Francisco and Mrs. Stanhope declared she would not have her charges growing up heathen, even if they were right smack in the middle of the most heathenish city that ever existed.

After their little services the elders were glad to sit in the sun or nap, but Minnie and Thomas were restless at doing nothing all day.

"Please, may we go for a walk?" begged Minnie. "I've not been anywhere except down the hill to the store. We'd like to explore the woods and fields a little."

"Well, a nice walk wouldn't be considered working on the Lord's Day, I suppose. Take your gun along, Minnie, and stay well away from town. And don't go over in the direction of Sydney Town. Those Sydney Ducks are—are—" Words to describe the Sydney Ducks failed her.

They promised to stay especially clear of Sydney Town, the section where the worst of San Francisco's roughnecks had settled. The Sydney Ducks were the worst troublemakers among the convicts who had been shipped to Australia from England, and Australia had allowed a number of them to ship to the gold fields, glad to get rid of them. Most of them came from Sydney, and existed in squalor in the group of filthy shacks known as Sydney Town. They made more by stealing than they might have made in the gold fields at the harder work of panning and digging. They marched into stores and took whatever they wanted, threatening to burn down the building if they were thwarted. So the frightened storekeepers let them take out whole sides of beef and bacon, and clothes, and money from the till, and felt they had got off easy when their stores were not burned.

It was a deplorable situation and many of the more permanent residents of San Francisco felt that something should be done about it. But the booming city was so new and raw, and so constantly changing, that there was little organization. Each one took care of himself as best he could and hoped the Sydney Ducks would not strike him next. So when Mrs. Stanhope called after them, "Now mind the Ducks, loves," she was warning them against a real danger. Yet the Ducks were not known to be nature lovers, so the chances of meeting them in the woods or fields was slim.

Minnie explained this all to Tom as they went down the other side of the hill, away from Sydney Town. The fields were dry and brown and would not turn green again until after the rainy season, for they were now into what would have been cold weather in Missouri and a real snow-and-ice winter in Massachusetts.

As they walked along a rabbit scuttled out from under a bramble bush and hopped across their path. Without even thinking, Minnie raised her gun and fired. The old gun had a powerful kick, and as usual she was knocked almost off her feet. But she had hit the rabbit. She was delighted and Tom was awed.

"I'll be blowed! You certainly shoot good for a girl."

"That was a good shot for a man," she retorted, sounding very much like Daisy. "We'll have fresh meat on the table again. Mrs. Stanhope'll make us a heavenly rabbit stew."

"One rabbit for six won't make much."

"Mrs. Stanhope will make it go around. She'll stretch it out with vegetables, and wait till you taste her gravy."

She was hungry already. She hesitated, though, when it came to picking up the rabbit. "I like target shooting better'n really hitting something alive. If it's not something we really need to eat, I won't shoot it."

"I know how you feel. A minute ago this was a lively little critter and now — " He picked up the rabbit and she smiled at him gratefully. He didn't laugh or call her a coward or make fun of her at all.

"If we need it for food, I figure it's all right," he said. "I don't know if I could shoot a person or not, even if my life depended on it. I just don't know."

The shot sounded loud in the quiet countryside and it startled more than the crows who fluttered into the air cawing and scolding. Tom and Minnie were still talking about the rabbit when two men stepped out from a group of trees ahead of them.

"Hey, that's a nice fat rabbit," one said. "Hand it over, kid. We'll have it for supper."

Minnie and Tom stood still. The men were mean and rough looking. "Ducks," said Minnie under her breath to Tom. He made no move to hand over the rabbit.

"Hand it over, matey," the man said again, impatiently.

"You heard him," said the other. "You know what we do to them as gits out of line." He grinned, a malicious grin that twisted his ugly face.

Tom answered, "This is our rabbit."

Minnie was frightened, but she tightened her grip on the gun and pointed it directly at the men, glad that she had reloaded immediately as her father had taught her.

One of the men laughed and said, "That's a big gun for such a pretty little girl — " he came toward them across the clearing. Tom's voice was suddenly harsh and commanding.

"Don't come a step nearer! Turn and get going! Get ready to fire, Minnie!"

The man laughed again and came on, "Look who's talkin'! A bloomin' little kid — "

"Shoot!" ordered Tom, and Minnie obeyed. A bullet kicked up dust and dry earth right at his feet, and his companion yelled, "Come on, Bill! Those damn kids mean it!"

The Ducks turned and leaped for the shelter of the trees.

Minnie and Tom could hear them crashing away down the hill. When there was not another sound, Tom said in his natural voice, "Let's get out of here, fast! Run!" They raced back the way they had come and only when they had gone a long way did they stop, panting and breathless.

"Tom, I was scared!"

"Well, you didn't act it."

"And you — you sounded like — I don't know what — like a grown man, giving out orders."

"I tried to. I tried to sound like Cap'n Cavendish's first mate yelling at a sailor. I kept praying my voice wouldn't crack."

"And I was praying I could hit the ground, or his foot, or something. I didn't want to kill him — "

"You did just fine. Now reload, just in case. Let's get this rabbit home and in the pot."

"Why wouldn't you give it to them?"

"That's what everyone has been doing with those Sydney Ducks. Then they just get bolder and do worse the next time. Cap'n Cavendish says on a ship you've got to stop trouble when it starts, and he's right."

"I guess he is, but I'd rather have someone else do the stopping. I guess I'm not very brave."

"Brave enough. You're cool as a cucumber when it counts. Now which way is home?"

They had rambled along across fields and through

little patches of woods in what had seemed to be a generally easterly direction. They were not in the least worried about getting lost, for they could see the sun and knew they must head west to get home. Somehow, though, they had been changing direction as they turned out to avoid bramble patches. They must have been making a circle that brought them clear around to Sydney Town to the south. They looked at the sun, now starting down the western sky, and headed for home.

Without discussing it, they both decided not to mention their brush with the Ducks. They might not be allowed out again. So they simply presented their rabbit, and Mrs. Stanhope hurried to get it ready for the pot. The stew turned out to be delicious and there was plenty for six.

"A nice change," declared Mrs. Stanhope. "You two can bring a rabbit anytime. I don't like to complain, but, Oh, I do get hungry for a good meat stew. Eggs and vegetables can get tiresome."

Shortly after that the rains began. They had been told about the winter rains, but they were not prepared for day after day after day of rainy weather. They had to tell their laundry customers to allow them more time for clothes to dry. They hung lines on the porch so that some of the moisture could blow out of sheets and shirts, and then did the final drying inside near the fire.

Tom worked extra hard chopping wood. Each day he brought in as big a pile of wood as he could so it would be dry enough to burn in a day or so.

They got used to living with lines of damp clothes crisscrossing the one-room house, and learned to step around the woodpiles. Everything felt damp and clammy, and their shoes were always wet even though they dried them each night by the stove.

Down in town the mud was unbelievable. Storekeepers threw down planks to make walking easier, but the planks soon sank into the mud. Wagons stuck and extra teams of horses and mules had to be hitched on to pull them out. A horse slipped and fell, and all the pulling and hauling did no good. The poor animal sank deeper and deeper, and finally a kind-hearted man shot it to put it out of its misery.

Daisy and Minnie found a way to get into the Emporium through the back door and so avoided the worst of the mire on the street. Even so, by the time they got inside, their skirts and shoes were muddy almost to the knees. They scraped off what they could, but it was impossible to get really clean, and anyway, the whole thing would be repeated in the evening.

Someone had the idea of dumping into the mud some of the unwanted cargo from the abandoned ships that lined the waterfront. Flour that was so rat-eaten it could not be used, tobacco, huge coils of rope, and finally even a load of cookstoves were dumped into the mud. They sank, leaving it almost as bad as ever. Tom saw the stoves being unloaded and ran to tell Daisy.

"You mean they're dumping perfectly good kitchen

cookstoves? That's horrible! Come on, let's see if we can get one!" They left their baking and ran out to see. "Don't dump them all," Daisy begged. "Let me have just one or two, please!"

The storekeepers said, "Nothing doing! We've got to get this filled up or business'll come to a standstill." Another said, "A miner fell in last night and drowned before he could get out. Drunk as a lord, he was, and never knew what happened to him." Still another said, "We could put in three shiploads of stoves and it wouldn't change anything — look at 'em sink. Save two out for the lady if she needs 'em."

They were very heavy, but somehow Daisy and Minnie and Tom managed to drag them back out of the way. Then Tom figured a way to take them apart, lids, stovepipes, oven doors, so the stoves were easier to handle. They got the pieces piled in the lean-to out of the rain.

"Not even rusted," Daisy gloated. "What a prize!" She wasn't sure what she needed them for, but said, "One of these days we'll find a use for them, you'll see."

It was the one bright spot in an otherwise dreary day, and only the fact that they were so busy saved them from being depressed and melancholy.

"We have to keep moving," said Tom. "If we stop for a minute, the mildew'll grow on us like it is on everything else."

In addition to everything else, the lean-to roof started to leak and Tom had scrounged some discarded packing crates for wood to mend it.

"Reckon I should pay him," said Mr. Haywood reluctantly.

"Reckon you should," answered Daisy. "It's your roof and your flour barrel the rain is leaking on. You couldn't find a carpenter to hire, nor afford to pay him if you found him, so pay the boy and stop grumping."

"You're a tough woman, Daisy Palmer." The old man hated to give in.

"One has to be a little tough to survive in this town," she retorted cheerfully, "otherwise there are millionaire storekeepers who would gladly take advantage of a poor helpless woman."

"Helpless!" he snorted. "The whole bunch of you are so far from helpless — and don't go hinting that I'm a millionaire. I'll have the Ducks in here, threatening me."

"We can handle the Ducks," said Daisy confidently. Tom and Minnie grinned at each other. They didn't think it was necessary to add that *they* already had.

11

A LONG LETTER came by ship from Aunt Addie. It was good to hear from her even though the letter was filled with complaints and reproaches. It had been written the day after Minnie and her father left.

DEAR PIERCE AND MINNIE,

I am still suffering with worry over your sudden departure, and especially from the shock of finding Minnie's letter in her empty bedroom. No words can describe my feelings. I will leave it to your imagination to guess what I have been through. What your dear little mother would have thought about this, Minnie, I dare not even try to think. I can only hope that you are safe and well and have not been eaten by wild animals or Indians and are not consorting with bad company. You know the stories we kept hearing about life in those dreadful mining camps.

Minnie, if you have not been eaten or scalped, you are to wear your sunbonnet at all times. I don't want you coming home weathered and sunburned, although you know I will welcome you both back no matter what terrible condition you may be in.

Today Banker Hanlon called on me, as you had requested him to do, Pierce, and told me that your entire bank account had been put at my disposal. That was kind and thoughtful, Pierce, but it would have been kinder still not to go. I need say no more. Banker Hanlon was sympathetic to my state and said emphatically that you had taken leave of your senses, both of you.

I have decided that it is my duty to keep an eye on the running of the livery stable. I still do not care for Mr. Tinker, but if duty calls, I will answer. I intend to see that the business is run right so that when you come home penniless and sorry, you will have a going business to help you recoup your losses. I do not for one minute expect you to come home rich, Pierce. The fabled gold mines are probably just that. If it were so easy, would we not have had at least one returning miner passing through St. Joseph with bags of gold? So far the traffic has been all one way. Banker Hanlon agrees with my estimate of the situation.

Rest assured that all is well cared for here. I wish I could be sure that the same is true for you in far off California, if indeed you will have reached there at all. I hope for the best but expect the worst.

Lovingly,

Your Aunt and Sister-in-law,

Adeline Hunter

Minnie could almost hear Aunt Addie's voice as she read the letter, and for a moment she felt homesick for her aunt and the pleasant house in St. Joseph. Only for a moment, though. Daisy called from the lean-to and she hurried out to help. There was no time for homesickness.

She had sent a long letter to Pa with Captain Cavendish. The two men might never meet, but the Captain had decided to head for Hangtown, and promised to find Mr. Weldon if he could. Not knowing exactly where Pa was and how he was doing was the hardest part. Letters came infrequently, sometimes several in a bunch written days and weeks apart. It was harder to get the news back to him. Supply wagons went regularly to the various settlements, but since Pa wasn't living at one of the so-called hotels, Minnie's letters did not always reach him.

She sighed and went on with her work. For the time being that was all she could do. One day she and her father would be together again. She just had to wait. She got a great deal of pleasure out of the way the jug had filled with money. That would be a real surprise for him. Mrs. Stanhope suggested that they hide their filled jugs and start others. They hid them well back in the cellar, behind some other dusty crocks and bottles. Thieves would not be likely to notice them there.

"They rush in and grab what they can and run out again, those Sydney Ducks! Although we must be fair, they're not the only ones. There was plenty of stealing before that bad lot arrived. Better we hide anything valuable and not take any chances."

The Stanhopes stayed up on the hill, washing and ironing and tending the garden. Mrs. Stanhope rejoiced that they did not have to make the daily trip into town. Tom took the eggs and the clean laundry, and brought back mail and more dirty clothes on his return home. A few times Minnie went with Tom to dip up sea water from the bay, but mostly her day was spent at the Emporium making hardtack. She would have liked to explore a little, but it wasn't safe, nor did she have the time.

The city of San Francisco was growing every day and it was more crowded than ever on the streets. The harbor was now quite cluttered with abandoned ships. A few — the beautiful new clippers — discharged their passengers and cargo and turned homeward before the crews could leave, but many other ships were deserted and swung lazily at anchor, inhabited mostly by great colonies of rats.

Between the rats that flourished everywhere and the mud and garbage in the streets, it was a wonder that San Francisco wasn't swept with epidemics, but perhaps the brisk sea air helped. For a city so crowded and filthy, most people stayed surprisingly well. There were outbreaks of fever now and then, but the illness was confined to the tents and shanties where living conditions were worst. The clear spring on their hilltop was pure and unpolluted, and they carried their own drinking water in their lunch pails.

It seemed a nuisance to Tom and Minnie to carry all that water, but Daisy insisted. She must have been right, for they all stayed well.

One of the other storekeepers along the waterfront, noticing the success of Mr. Haywood's bakery, set up a similar workshop behind his store. But all the bakers he hired lasted only a few days while they made enough money for a pickaxe and panning basin. Then they lit out for the gold fields. The customers soon learned the Haywood's hardtack was fit to eat, clean, consistantly browned, not burned nor half-baked. In the end the competitor gave up in disgust, and Daisy and Minnie and Tom had the field all to themselves.

One day Mr. Dan Lawrence, the man with the ruffled shirts, the one who had been the first laundry customer, asked to speak to Daisy.

"Dan Lawrence, the gambler, wants to talk to you," said Mr. Haywood, all agog with curiosity.

"Talk's free," said Daisy. "But I can't stop what I'm doing. Ask him to come back here."

Mr. Lawrence came back to the lean-to. Mr. Haywood hung around to see what it was all about, but to his disappointment, the bell on the front door tinkled and he had to leave to wait on a customer.

"You didn't miss anything world-shaking," Daisy told him later, amused at his interest. "He asked me to prepare the way for a visit to Mrs. Stanhope tomorrow. He's afraid of her gun."

"Now why would Dan Lawrence want to talk to Hannah Stanhope," wondered Mr. Haywood.

"Maybe he wants more starch in his shirts," giggled Minnie.

"No, seriously, what could he want?"

"He didn't choose to confide in me," said Daisy.

"If he wants to take the laundry business away from me, remind Mrs. Stanhope that if it hadn't been for me and my store, she'd never — "

Daisy laughed. "So that's what is worrying you! You and your fifty cents per piece! Well, it is a nice profit for doing nothing. No wonder you're concerned. I suppose if that's the case, you'll know soon enough."

"Let me know as soon as you find out," he urged. "Maybe if that's the problem, I could take a mite less — say forty-five cents?"

"Mrs. Stanhope will be the one to inform you of her decision if it concerns you at all," said Daisy primly. "Now why don't you run along and tend to your store, Mr. Haywood? You don't want to slow us down, now, do you?" He left, grumbling that Daisy Palmer was acting mighty ungrateful. "Remember, I made you, and I can unmake you. It's my flour and my stove and my store!"

Daisy and Tom and Minnie were just as curious as Mr. Haywood, but they never would have admitted it to him. Mrs. Stanhope and the girls were even more curious. They couldn't imagine what the gambler could want.

"If he wasn't satisfied with his shirts, he'd just send word, wouldn't he? He wouldn't climb all the way up here for that, would he?"

126

"I scorched his shirttail one day last week," confessed Ruby, "but only a little, and not where it would show. It can't be that."

They had to wait until the next day to find out. It was Sunday so all of them were sitting out on the porch when they saw the handsome elegantly dressed gentleman toiling up the hill. He raised his silk hat and waved it as a sign of friendship, and Mrs. Stanhope waved him on.

"Should we leave?" asked Daisy. "Maybe he wants to talk to you in private."

"No, indeed," Mrs. Stanhope answered firmly. "If it's the laundry business, and I can't imagine what else he'd have to talk to me about, I need you to figure quick in your head so I won't get cheated. Anyway, we're all one family and we can all hear whatever he's got to say."

Mr. Lawrence opened the gate cautiously, making sure that Mrs. Stanhope wasn't aiming her gun at him. She waved again to show that she wasn't armed at the moment, and chuckled. "It guess I got 'em all pretty scared," she said. "The word has got around."

Mr. Lawrence was most courteous. He bowed to all the ladies and asked after their health and admired the magnificent view. Finally he finished with his politenesses and got down to the matter that was on his mind.

"Mrs. Stanhope, word has come to me that your two lovely daughters sing and play charmingly." She stiffened her back and sat up very straight. "Now,

please hear me out before you say no, and I beg of you to keep in mind that what I intend is a wholly respectable establishment, no drinking, no gambling, a place where any minister of the gospel might attend and approve. I am now having built and will soon open an opera house in Rich Bar where I will present only uplifting and edifying performances. It will do a great service in improving the manners and morals of those poor benighted men, the miners, who are so far from the cultural benefits of home."

Mrs. Stanhope snorted. "Those poor benighted miners are also loaded with gold, which you would be very happy to get your hands on, Mr. Lawrence. I don't imagine the Opera House will be free."

"There will, of course, be an admission fee. The hall itself will be a magnificent edifice and very expensive to build. It will be so elegant that it will have a refining effect on the audience, not to mention performers of the highest type of artistry."

"And you would like Ruby and Pearl to play and sing at your Opera House? The answer, Mr. Lawrence, is no."

"You haven't heard how much I plan to pay for the music made by such beautiful unspoiled young ladies, like fragile flowers. One hundred dollars per performance, Mrs. Stanhope, and you should know that when the miners approve they often throw bags of gold on the stage — all of this would belong to you and your daughters. And I will guarantee the comfort and luxury of your living quarters, with all possible concern for your privacy and safety. All for a short performance each evening."

"No."

"There will be other artistes passing through and adding to the elegance of the offerings, so your daughters will play and sing for less than an hour each time. In addition I want you to know that Rich Bar has become a really civilized town — "

"If I planned to put my daughters on the stage, I could have built one myself out of packing crates long before ths. We could have two performances a day right down at the water front. Maybe we could catch the miners before they get to your gambling house or Emma's dance hall."

"You won't even sleep on the idea?"

"I'd a sight rather sleep on a bed of thistles. Sleeping on it wouldn't make any difference."

"Ma," said Ruby timidly, "if you sat right there on the stage — "

"No," said Mrs. Stanhope. "Good day, Mr. Lawrence."

"You could sit on the stage with your gun," offered Mr. Lawrence eagerly.

"No," said Mrs. Stanhope.

He stood up, bowed to each one of them and put on his high silk hat. "It was such a good idea," he said sadly. "Good day, Mrs. Stanhope. If you change your mind, you'll find I'm still eager to do business."

They watched him go down the hill. No one said

anything. Then Pearl asked, "Ma, mightn't it be sort of an adventure?"

"The kind of adventure we don't need," she answered firmly. "We've got enough adventure right here."

"Sometimes Pearl and I wonder if there isn't more to life than just washing and starching and ironing someone else's shirts and petticoats," said Ruby.

"No need to discuss it any more, girls. I've made up my mind."

The very next day Tom brought home a letter from Rich Bar along with the day's bundle of dirty clothes.

"It's from Josephus," said Mrs. Stanhope. "Girls, it's from your father." She dried her hands on her apron and tore open the letter eagerly. Pearl straightened up from the wash tub and listened. Ruby finished the shirt she was ironing and put the iron back on the stove to heat.

"Well, what does he say, Ma?" she asked after a moment. "He's all right, isn't he?"

"No, he's not," answered their mother, her voice trembling. "He's not all right. He's not all right at all. The bending and stooping in the stream has given him bad rheumatiz — and his poke's been stolen!"

"Oh, poor Pa!"

"His whole poke — all the gold he's dug and panned so far — almost enough for a good farm. He was just thinking it might be wise to bring it back here for us to guard, and some low-lifer stole it!

Everything! Burro and tools and his food and all the gold. He woke up and found it all gone. Oh, Josephus, why did I ever let you go without me? It's all my fault!"

Daisy put her arm around the little woman's shoulder. "Now, now," she said, "don't cry, don't cry." Ruby and Pearl ran to hug their mother.

"Ma, it's not your fault — it's the way things are in those awful towns! Pa'll find more gold. There must be lots there. Don't give up hope."

Mrs. Stanhope pulled herself together.

"This calls for a lot more'n hope, girls. We've got to act. We'll go to Rich Bar and take care of your Pa. If he's got rheumatiz, he's got no business standing in ice-cold mountain water panning for gold. He'll catch his death of cold and won't be able to enjoy the farm he's been working so hard to get. I've got to go and take care of him. Let me get my wits together and do some planning."

She sat down at the table and put her head in her hands. They all stood quietly waiting for her to tell her plans. When she finally spoke she seemed her old self, brisk and confident.

"Daisy, can you manage here with Minnie and Tom if we run out on you? I think our place is with Josephus, but I hate to go off and leave you to manage all alone."

"We can manage fine. You must do what you think is right and don't worry about us at all."

"Then, Tom, you go to Dan Lawrence's gambling house. Don't go in, just stand at the door; I promised Captain Cavendish I'd keep you out of harm. Tell Mr. Lawrence that if his offer includes a place for Josephus and the cow and horse and the pen of chickens — not Josephus in with the cow, Mr. Lawrence'll understand; if he can provide that, we'll go. We're going to Rich Bar, and we'll stay only until spring comes. By then we'll have plenty for a beautiful farm up in Oregon, maybe, and we can start all over again. Girls, I'll sit on that stage with my gun across my knees, and no miner had better say a single rough word. You'll play and sing only the hymns and pretty songs you already know — no dance hall pieces, nothing I'd be ashamed to have you sing at a nice party at home. If Mr. Lawrence wants you on those terms, maybe no harm'll come of it. Anyway, I've got to take a chance. I've got to stand by my Josephus when he needs me."

12

I⊤ WAS HARD to say good-bye to the Stanhopes. In
the few months they had shared the farmhouse on
the top of the hill, they had all come to feel like
family. Ruby and Pearl and Minnie cried, and Tom
did his best not to, for he felt he was too old for such
babyishness. To a motherless boy, Mrs. Stanhope
had given the closest to real mothering that he had
had in a long time. Seeing his distress, Daisy Palmer must have felt she should try to take Mrs. Stanhope's place, for she put an arm around each of the
children and hugged them tight as the wagon drove
off down the steep and rutted hill road.

Mrs. Stanhope sat up very straight on the wagon
seat with her fierce-looking unloaded gun across
her knees. Ruby drove and Pearl sat in the middle,
turning around to wave until they were out of sight.
They could not have gone very fast even if the road
had been better, for the cow was tied to the back of
the wagon, and their speed had to be matched to hers.
All their belongings were packed in the wagon under a

canvas cover. They had left room in the wagon for three blanket beds. It would not be comfortable, but it would be drier than the ground for the nights they would have to spend on the road to Rich Bar.

The chickens were in their crate fastened to the side of the wagon. Mrs. Stanhope had left half the hens behind.

"I wish I could leave 'em all for you," she said. "I'd feel a mite better about going off and leaving you like this. But we'll need a couple of hens and the rooster to start the flock again when we get our farm. God willing, that'll be this spring, and maybe we can even get part of a crop in yet this year. Anyway, these old girls I'm leaving behind will lay for a while yet. When they slacken off, don't hesitate to eat them. They'll stew up just lovely."

Mrs. Stanhope had left the furniture, what there was of it, behind. "It's all homemade, anyhow, and Cousin Charlie, wherever he is, certainly won't mind if you use it. Now don't you worry about us and Josephus. We'll be fine. And I'll try not to worry about you three. Minnie, don't forget to carry your gun everywhere you go. I hope you never have to use it, but be alert."

With many last minute admonitions about keeping their feet dry, which was impossible, and keeping their spirits up, which was more likely, Mrs. Stanhope left.

It was very quiet without them. Daisy read out of the Bible as was their custom on Sunday morning, and they sang a hymn or two. But without Ruby's violin and the Stanhope voices, the songs didn't sound like much. They spent the rest of the day not saying much, each thinking lonesome thoughts.

Early Monday morning they were up again and ready to start a new week of work. They missed the rooster's crowing, but habit woke them anyway.

"What about the laundry?" asked Tom. "Do you think we could manage both jobs?"

Daisy thought about it. "I'm afraid not. It was a full-time job for the three Stanhopes, and goodness knows we have enough to do at the store. No, I guess not. We'll return all the clean clothes and tell the customers the laundry is out of business."

Mr. Lawrence was upset when he heard the news. "I'm delighted, of course, that Mrs. Stanhope agreed to let her daughters appear at the Opera House. I just never thought it through — that if I gained two singers I'd lose my clean shirts. The girls at Emma's place will be in an uproar."

"They could wash and iron their own petticoats," suggested Daisy. "Maybe they'll do your shirts, too."

"Heavens, no! They're not the home kind of girls. They wouldn't stoop to doing laundry."

"That's too bad," said Daisy coldly. "They stoop to almost anything else, don't they? At any rate, you'll have to look elsewhere, Mr. Lawrence." She turned her back on him and went to work rolling out more hardtack.

He stared at her. "You're a mighty pretty girl, Miss Palmer. Can you dance or sing?"

She answered without turning around. "If I could, I wouldn't work for you, Mr. Lawrence. I'd open my own Opera House."

"Highty-tighty," he laughed. "I'll bet you would, and rake in all the profit, too, Daisy."

"Profit isn't the only thing I think about. I have a good use for the money I'm making. And the name is Miss Palmer."

He laughed again, and left with his pile of ruffled shirts.

"A gambler sure dresses fancy, doesn't he?" asked Tom. "He must be a millionaire, or almost."

"Scum of the earth, rich or poor." She dismissed him shortly. "I'll be needing more water, Tom."

Their days went on much as before, except that they no longer carried laundry back and forth, and at night had no one with whom to discuss all the events of the day. There was plenty going on. The Sydney Ducks were growing bolder and bolder. Miners were robbed in broad daylight, and store-keepers handed over their choicest goods for fear of reprisal from the outlaws. They heard that some of the mining camps had set up crude courts and were dealing out stern justice to the worst of the law breakers. But in San Francisco there were too few permanent residents to regulate things, and the people who were passing through had little interest unless they happened to be the ones who were robbed and beaten.

At night Daisy fastened and locked the shutters over the windows and barred both the doors. They kept the chickens in the shed and brought their crate inside at night. Minnie hated it. She liked the window open so that the wind, even if chilly, could blow through; and without getting out of bed in the morning she could see the sky and tell what kind of a day it was. Tom missed his bed in the hayloft, but Daisy said she would feel safer if they were all under one roof. So he slept in the bed that had been Ruby's and Pearl's, and Daisy hung a curtain beside it to give him privacy.

Tom brought in a supply of water before it got dark so they did not have to go out again, and all three slept lightly. If the house settled and shifted or a board creaked, Minnie reached for her gun. It was not a pleasant way to live, nor a restful one.

The townspeople appointed policemen, but the Ducks terrified the officers of the law and threatened them. Mr. Haywood refused to tell the Ducks where he kept his money hidden, and his house was burned right over his head.

He took several blankets out of stock for a mattress and slept on the floor in the Emporium.

"They'll burn this place over my dead body," he said grimly.

Daisy answered soberly, "It might come to just that. Keep a path clear to the door, Mr. Haywood, and don't sleep too soundly."

A group of three Ducks came into the Emporium one day and demanded food. Before they even knew whether Mr. Haywood would give it to them or not, they started to turn over barrels and boxes and to

139

pull things off the shelf. Back in the lean-to they heard the crash and Mr. Haywood's frightened, angry voice.

"You get out of here, you low-lifes!" he shouted. Tom started in to the store, but Daisy grabbed his shirt. "Don't," she begged. "I'll go, but you and Minnie stay — "

"Please, Daisy, they may hurt him — "

While Daisy was holding Tom, Minnie grabbed her gun and ran through the door. One of the Ducks had lifted Mr. Haywood right off the floor and was starting to shake him as a puppy does a bone.

"Where'd you hide it, moneybags?" One of them asked. "Where's all the money you've been making, huh? Tell us, or we'll squeeze it out of you!"

Minnie had scooted along behind the counter. They were so busy with Mr. Haywood that they did not notice her until she popped up from behind the counter.

"Let go of him!" She was so scared that her voice quavered, but her gun did not. Tom broke loose from Daisy and ran, and she followed on his heels. The Ducks turned around, surprised. The one who was holding Mr. Haywood stopped his shaking, but he did not put him down. The storekeeper's face was almost purple, for his stiff collar was cutting off his breath.

"Let go of him!" Minnie said again. Tom and Daisy were at her side now. One man laughed, but one of the other two said, "Wait, ain't that the kid who shot at us before? She means it! She ain't foolin'."

The laugher started for Minnie, reaching for the gun. She whirled around and pressed it right against the ribs of Mr. Haywood's tormentor.

"Lay a hand on her and she'll blow your friend to bits!" said Tom.

"She's never missed yet," added Daisy. "Let go of him and get out of here!" Daisy grabbed up a heavy pickaxe and advanced on them. They took one look at her stoney white face and started to back away.

The Ducks were impressed enough to leave, but they called back, "Watch your gold, old moneybags! We'll get you yet."

Inside the Emporium, Mr. Haywood was taking deep breaths and gasping. Daisy leaned weakly against the counter. Minnie found that the gun was wobbling and shaking in her hand. She could not have hit anything with any accuracy. Only Tom was fairly calm. When Mr. Haywood could talk he said, "Can't thank you — enough — they'd have choked me — if — you hadn't come in — "

Daisy said, "I told the children not to come, but I'm glad they did. The Ducks will be back again, I'm afraid. They're determined to get your money."

"Well, they won't. And wherever you three are keeping yours, you'd better be sure it's safe. You've all worked too hard to have the Ducks take it away from you. For two cents I'd pack up here and leave.

I'm tired of sleeping on the floor and living to outwit those no-goods. I'm beginning to think the money's not worth it."

"Speaking of money," Daisy said shakily, "let's all get back to work. While we've been in here acting like heroes, the stovepipe may have set the wall on fire."

One batch of hardtack had burned to a crisp, but the wall was still damp and not even smoking. They worked as swiftly and steadily as always, but all were thoughtful. When they stopped to eat the lunch Daisy had packed, she talked about their hidden money.

"I don't like the idea that the house is empty all day long. Those Ducks know we are here — they could tear the house apart at their leisure and sooner or later they'd find those crocks. We'll have to think of someplace else."

They worked quietly all afternoon, and as usual their output was sold out as fast as they made it. The thin hard sheets of bread would keep indefinitely. Even if it got wet and soggy it could be dried over a campfire, or fried crisp in a frying pan. There was a steady stream of miners coming in to the store in response to the sign, "Fresh Baked Hardtack! No Worms or Bugs! Fit to Eat!"

Some were new fortune-seekers outfitting themselves for their first trip to the gold fields. Others were sadder and wiser miners, sober now after they had spent all their hard-won treasure at the rows of gambling houses and dance halls. No matter, they all needed hardtack to keep them going, and business was brisk.

Daisy collected their pay as usual and portioned it out to each one. For once Mr. Haywood didn't grumble that Daisy was a skinflint or a hard bargainer. He smiled at them all gratefully, and wonder of wonders, asked if they would like a piece of beef jerky for a change in diet. "Free," he added.

It would have been better with milk, but Daisy managed to concoct a gravy with water, and it tasted delicious.

That night before they settled down · to sleep, Daisy bolted the doors and shutters as usual, and piled the chairs and the table against the doors.

"It won't keep the Ducks out," she said, "but it'll make enough of a crash to wake us if they do come in. Tomorrow we're going to find a better place for our money."

Minnie finally fell asleep that night, but not for a long time. She could hear Tom's breathing behind the curtain. Daisy slept restlessly, tossing and turning and occasionally moaning a little.

The threat that hung over them, indeed over all the city, had taken away most of the zest they had felt in meeting the challenges of the rough, raw, new town. Now their day's work was only tiring, not exciting, and the money they were earning was a burden instead of a reward.

Minnie finally slept. The moon rose and shone

from behind the clouds, but the bright moonlight did not penetrate the boarded-up and barricaded house on the hill.

13

THEY LOCKED UP the next morning, leaving everything as safe as they could and walked down the
hill to the Emporium. None of the three looked
forward to another day of hard work and another
fearful restless night. They passed the quiet tent
camp, now occupied by a new group of miners who
would stay there only long enough to get outfitted for
their trip to the gold fields. The sun was not yet up
and the tent dwellers were still asleep.

Their reluctant steps quickened as they came to the
bend in the road where they could see over all the
waterfront street. A column of smoke rose straight
up in the calm morning air.

"Isn't that — it's the Emporium!" said Tom, starting to run. Daisy and Minnie hiked up their skirts
and ran after him as fast as they could. It was the
Emporium, or what was left of it.

The front part of the store was entirely burned out
and most of what was left standing was scorched and
smoldering. The back wall of the store and the lean-

to were still standing, several rafters and a supporting post were blackened but still there. The roof was gone.

Mr. Haywood was poking around in the ruins, pulling out one boot here, a charred axe handle there, a bolt of cloth that was still usable, an unopened barrel of molasses that had somehow escaped. The old man looked dazed and forlorn, wandering around what yesterday had been his busy, prosperous, well-stocked establishment.

"The Ducks?" asked Daisy. He nodded. "They were determined to find my money. They were threatening me, tearing up the floorboards and ripping boxes open, when one of them tipped over the lamp. The fire went so fast — " he shook his head. "Those thugs let go of me and started to grab bacon, tools, whatever they could get. I tried to throw water on the flames but it was no use. They took what they could and ran, and I soon saw I'd have to get out, too. Some of the neighbors tried to help — too late, too late. Lucky it was a land breeze or the rest of it'd be gone too, although what's the use of one wall and a lean-to? I'm finished." He shook his head sadly.

"You can rebuild; we'll help you," said Tom.

"No use. They'd burn me out again, and it'd take months to get restocked, anyway. No, I'm finished here. A few minutes more and they would have found where I hid the money and that'd be gone, too. I am lucky, I guess. I have my passage money home and a nice little cash box, enough to keep me the rest of my life. I'm going to leave this place while I still have something to take with me. But oh, the waste, the awful waste!" He put his head in his hands and closed his eyes.

Minnie felt really sorry for him. The Emporium had been his whole life — he had no wife or family — and now it was gone. Daisy patted his shoulder sympathetically until he had control of himself again. Minnie and Tom dug around in the debris to see if they could rescue anything.

147

Finally Mr. Haywood said, "What will you do, Daisy?"

"I think we can still use the lean-to. It's in pretty good shape. I'll make a new sign as soon as we're open for business again."

"Daisy, they'll burn you out, too. You won't even know about it up on the hill, and you certainly can't live in that shed and sit up all night protecting the place. You'd better leave, too."

"We can't," she said. "Even if I wanted to leave, I couldn't. I'm responsible for Tom and Minnie until Mr. Weldon and Captain Cavendish come home. I couldn't leave, and what's more, I don't want to! I'm not going to be run out by those hoodlums! Just let me think — "

"You can think all you want to. Goodness knows I did. There's no way to outwit the Ducks."

"There must be!"

He shook his head wearily and got up to join Tom and Minnie in their search for anything that had not burned or been spoiled by the fire. They hauled out pails and cooking pans that were blackened with soot but still good. A whole pile of brass washing pans for panning gold were as good as new when they were wiped off.

Minnie reported triumphantly that the flour barrels were charred a little but the flour inside was as good as new. It didn't even smell smokey. And a whole batch of leather harness straps were still hanging from one of the remaining rafters.

"There's enough here to make a start, Mr. Haywood," she said. "The smoked herring is fine, just a little more smoked, that's all."

"No," he said. "My mind's made up. I'm going. It's all yours, Daisy and Tom and Minnie, a present from me; so do what you want with it, but count me out. I'm going back on the next ship out. Back to Baltimore. If I have any luck, there might be a ship leaving today. I'll have no trouble getting a return passage."

"Well, we're not through," said Daisy decisively. "I don't intend to leave until I've enough money to start a school. Not here, maybe, but somewhere back East. And I've a plan. Sit down, all of you and tell me what you think."

"I can tell you right now," said Mr. Haywood, sitting on a barrel. "Whatever your plan is, it won't work. You'd all be better off leaving messages for the Captain and Minnie's Pa and booking passage with me. Much better off."

"Be quiet and listen," said Daisy, "and don't any of you make up your mind until you hear me out. What do you say we move down from the hill, find a new place to live, and start up our business all over again? If the flour isn't spoiled, that's a small fortune right there. The stoves are fine, so we can go on with the hardtack, and we can have a sale and get rid of all the store goods. We'll find a place where the Ducks can't sneak up on us, and we'll guard our home and the store at the same time."

"But where?"

That was the problem. There seemed to be no

answer to that one. Thinking hard, Minnie looked out over the still-quiet waterfront street. An idea was bouncing around in her head. If only she could catch it and tie it down —

"Could we live on one of those ships?" she asked timidly. "It would be hard for the Ducks to sneak up on us there." The idea seemed too outlandish to be taken seriously, but Daisy gave a little yelp of excitement.

"That's it!" she said. "Minnie, that's it! Why can't we make one of those docked ships into a store? Cut a door in the hull and set up shop right inside. Those hulks aren't fit to go to sea, now, but they are plenty good enough to make us a good safe store and living quarters. There'd be only one door and we could make that strong enough to keep out intruders. We'll have farther to go for drinking water, but we'll probably find some water casks that we could fill once a day. What do you say, partners? Shall we try it?"

It was all so sudden that no one could think of what to say. Daisy went on, "And if we don't try it, what will we do? I'm so weary of living like a prisoner in the farmhouse, all boarded up and creeping around in fear of our lives up there."

Tom and Minnie were enthusiastic. Mr. Haywood still shook his head. "I'll stay long enough to help you get set up, but I'm afraid you'll end up no better off than I am."

"Let's not cross that bridge until we come to it. Which ship shall we choose?" They walked along the street in the rosy early morning light and looked long and hard at each one. Some were so high out of the water that a door cut in the hull would lead into the lower part of the ship.

"We need one that's low in the water," said Tom. "Not that one. The poor old *Sea Rover* is too far gone — the planks are rotting, see? And not the *Nellie Blanchford*, or the *Skylark*. There's one that looks likely, the *Golden Venture*. Must not even have been unloaded before the crew skipped — see how low it is in the water?"

"The *Golden Venture!* We'll take it! The name's a lucky sign, don't you think?" asked Daisy.

"You're going to need more than lucky signs, Daisy. But it is a likely looking ship, if you're determined to go ahead with this. She's in good shape above the water line at any rate. I still say you're mad."

As long as Minnie and Tom were willing to go ahead, Daisy paid no attention to Mr. Haywood's gloomy remarks. They hurried back to the ruins of the Emporium to find the tools Tom had used to build a storage shelf in the lean-to. The saw and hammer were untouched by the fire, and they found a keg of nails in the ashes.

"See?" Daisy was determinedly cheerful. "It must be that we're meant to go ahead with this. Everything we need is right here waiting for us."

Back at the *Golden Venture*, they stared up at the bowsprit and figurehead that loomed above.

151

"How do we get on it?"

"There's a rope hanging over the side. I can go up easy."

"Oh, be careful, Tom. Are you sure?"

They watched nervously while he ran and leaped for the rope above his head. He missed once, twice, but on the third leap he got a good grip on it. He swung there a moment and then reached cautiously up, hand over hand, until he could wrap his legs around the end of the rope. Then it went faster, and in a few moments he was pushing off from the deck railing. He swung out, and on the return swing dropped lightly down on the deck. Minnie breathed easier then, and loosened her grip on Daisy's hand.

"I — I don't think I could do that — "

"We won't have to," Daisy was confident. "We'll cut a hole in the ship and go in that way. Tom," she called, "go down to where you are level with the wharf and knock on the wall. Then we'll know where to start sawing."

He nodded, waved and disappeared. They crowded close to the bow so they could hear him when he pounded. Finally they just barely heard a faint tapping. Daisy grabbed up a piece of mud from the street and marked the place where the sound had come from. In a couple of minutes Tom's head popped up. He leaned over the railing and shouted, "Could you hear me? Well, then, that's where the door should go. I'm going to find the carpenter's shop. I'll get a tool to break through, and we can make an opening."

Again they waited anxiously. Time had passed faster than they had realized. The town was stirring, shops were opening, customers began to hurry along the street, dodging mudholes and carts. The little group moved back out of the way. Daisy made them try to look as if they were having just a friendly conversation, for until the plan had been put into action, she wasn't anxious for anyone to know what they were up to.

She was so excited that her pink cheeks were even pinker. Her blue calico work dress had faded to a soft, most becoming color. A smudge of soot was on her face and her hands were black from handling the smokey things in the store. Even so, she had never looked prettier. Many going by looked at her with interest, and some made remarks, but she didn't notice.

When Tom appeared again he dropped a rope ladder over the side and came down as easily as coming down stairs. He had news that didn't sound promising.

"The *Golden Venture* is a good ship, all right. Too good for us, I'm afraid. We could work for days and not break through these timbers. They're thick, and hard as iron. I couldn't do more than flake off a few chips with the tools I could find."

Daisy swallowed hard. She was very disappointed, but not ready to give up yet. "Let me try that ladder," she said, and handed the hammer and saw to Minnie. She looped up her long full skirt, tucked it firmly into her waistband and was part way up the ladder before they knew what she was planning to do. At the top she climbed over the railing and stood on the deck. Then she stepped over the railing and backed down. The return trip was harder, for she had to make sure her foot was firmly on the rung before she put her weight on it. But when she stepped off on the ground she was beaming.

"We don't have to cut through at all," she said excitedly. "We can build a shelter easily up there on the deck, no problem there, and that will be the bakery. We'll have a table down here for the store, and we'll lower the hardtack on a rope. At night we can draw up the ladder and keep intruders away! It's perfect! Let's all go up and go to work!"

Mr. Haywood was convinced at last. "It's certainly a peculiar way to run a store, but then everything in San Francisco is peculiar. Let's go! Tom, you go first and help me over the rail. That's the part I'm not sure of."

Tom suggested that they saw an opening through the rail to make it easier to get on board. Before long they were all on board the *Golden Venture*. Tom got lumber from the carpenter's shop and in a short time they had a crude building nailed together. It wasn't much to look at, but few buildings in San Francisco were. It was every bit as weathertight as the lean-to had been, and had more room in it.

Tom and Mr. Haywood went back to the Emporium to get the back door of the lean-to. They fitted it snugly into the doorway.

"When it rains we'll drape a sail over the whole thing and the wind and rain will be kept out," said Tom.

When that much was finished they took time to examine the captain's cabin. It was an elegant room with wardrobes and storage places and even book-shelves. Daisy gasped. It was the first time she had seen a row of books since she left Boston. "I can unpack my books! Glory be!"

The passenger cabin next door was a little smaller, but plenty roomy enough to suit Tom and Mr. Haywood. The storekeeper was so pleased he was beginning to weaken.

"I might just stay on a few days more and help you get started," he said. "I just might wait a little while until you're settled in and established."

Daisy smiled at him gratefully. "We'd be so glad if you would. No one in the world knows more about storekeeping than you do."

"Flattery will get you nowhere," he said grumpily. "I don't intend to hang around here long, you understand, and I won't do it for nothing, neither."

He sounded more like his old, grouchy, money-grabbing self, and somehow that was very comforting.

14

THEY PLANNED to bring their few personal belongings and the chickens down from the farm. They
could do it in two trips if the heavy crocks of money
could be wrapped in sheets and quilts. When they
came down at dusk, no one would even notice. In
the meantime, they would carry the stove parts and
the barrels of flour from the lean-to in the two-
wheeled cart that was still tipped up in back of the
lean-to.

"We can be so glad that the wind was from the
land last night, otherwise everything would be gone.
We must be grateful for many things."

"Save your gratitude until we see how things work
out, Daisy," warned Mr. Haywood. "This may be the
biggest failure we've ever seen."

"Never!" declared Daisy.

"We'll make it work," said Minnie. "We can do it
if we try."

It took awhile to cart the stoves and flour and
Daisy's makeshift work table and equipment up the

crowded street to the *Golden Venture*, and it took even longer to haul them up to the deck. There was plenty of good strong rope aboard and Tom knew the places where it would probably be kept. He rigged up a pulley, and after a long struggle everything was up on the ship.

By that time all four of them were thoroughly tired as well as dirty. Tom and Minnie carried water from back of the Emporium and they washed just enough of their hands and faces to be reasonably clean for lunch. It seemed years ago, but it was only last night that Daisy had packed their lunch, and it was only this morning that they had carried that lunch down the hill, to find the Emporium in smoking ruins.

They shared their lunch with Mr. Haywood and washed down the dryish bread with plenty of water. It wasn't really enough, after all their hard work, but it would have to do.

Daisy investigated the ship's galley, but decided against using it. "Phew!" she said. "Small and smelly and dark, and hot, I should imagine, when the stove is going. No, we're better off cooking up here on deck where the breeze can blow the heat away. We can use an old sail for an awning if the sun gets too hot."

While they ate and rested Daisy was planning. "There's no need for customers to come up here at all. We'll have the fire sale down on the wharf, and then we can open the bakery again. Customers can give their hardtack orders to Mr. Haywood and he can send the money up on a rope — we'll find a bag or basket somewhere — and we'll lower the package of bread. Unless it is someone we know, we just won't allow anyone to come and see how we are set up."

That is what they decided, and they spent the rest of the afternoon pawing through the charred remains of the Emporium to find anything that might be usable. Plenty of friends and acquaintances stopped by to tell Mr. Haywood they were sorry, and also to see what they could find in the ruins. He thanked them all for their concern, and made it clear that he had plans to use anything that hadn't been burned.

"Come tomorrow to the big sale," he urged. "You'll find bargains a plenty."

By evening they were tired and smokey-smelling and blackened almost beyond recognition.

"No one will notice us now," laughed Daisy. "We look as grubby and dirty as any goldminer — as grubby as Ducks, even. But we won't clean up until after we've made the trips to the farmhouse. We'll fade right into the shadows."

The shadows were growing long as one by one they came down the rope ladder. When they were on the wharf, Tom said, "What's to keep some Ducks from going up the ladder while we're gone? They may have noticed what we're up to, you know."

"That ladder looks like an invitation," agreed Mr. Haywood, "and the Ducks'll come even without an invitation. No need to make it easy for them."

"Then you stay here, Mr. Haywood," said Daisy. "Go back up on the ship and pull the ladder up behind

158

you, and don't let it down until we come back."

"You're sure you'll be all right?"

"Who would bother us when Minnie's carrying her gun? We'll be back soon, before it gets really dark," said Daisy.

On the first trip down they took Daisy's satchels of books and the few staples they had in the cupboard. As they toiled up the hill for the last time, Tom puffed, "It'll seem strange, not going up to the farm every night."

"Not as strange as having the Ducks burn us out," said Daisy. "You'll see; this arrangement will be better."

They stripped the beds and used the sheets and blankets to wrap their extra clothes in. They tied the crocks of money inside the bundles, too. Daisy took the crate of hens and all the grain, and shifting her load from one arm to the other, decided she could manage it. She bolted the shutters and the back door, and locked the front door securely. It wouldn't keep out determined intruders, but would delay them a trifle.

They had started out the gate when a thought struck her. "Tom, Minnie! What will happen when Captain Cavendish and Mr. Weldon return and find us gone, and the Emporium burned down? They'll be worried, and where would they begin to look for you? Wait, we've got to leave a note."

"If the Ducks read it, they'll know where to find us," objected Tom.

"They'll find out soon enough, anyway. We can't

run a business and keep it a secret. Besides, I doubt
if most of the Ducks can read."

Daisy set down the crate of complaining hens and
opened a bundle to rummage for a pencil and paper.
She wrote a note addressed to Captain Cavendish and
Minnie's father telling them that the children could
be found on the *Golden Venture*, across the street
from Mr. Lawrence's gambling house, The Red Lion.
Then on another sheet she added a postscript intended
for any of the Ducks who might be able to read.

The money bag is buried deep,
Under where the potatoes sleep.
Thirty paces to the east, five to the south, and eight
    to the west,
Dig wherever you think is best.

She added a large black cross to mark the spot, and
measurements and arrows, enough to excite any
Duck who might think he had found a map of buried
treasure.

"I hope they take the bait and dig up the entire
vegetable garden. I'd like to see some of those
ruffians work for their gold for a change." She
went back and stuck the pages under a loose board
on the porch so they wouldn't blow away, and then
took up her load again.

They took one last look at the little house that had
been their home, and turned away, down the road to
the water front. It wasn't easy to walk with the road
so rough and rocky, and the sun already going down.
They stumbled along as best they could, setting down

their burdens from time to time when they needed to rest. Minnie still carried her gun. It was a habit, now, but she would have had a hard time shooting it if the need had arisen. Her arms ached with carrying the awkward bundle of quilts and clothes and money, and her gun was very much in the way. She thought her arms would drop off if she had to go one more step, but it was not a time for complaints. The others were loaded just as heavily, so she staggered on.

"Never — seemed — so far before," panted Tom. He was carrying their dishes and pans and the remains of their food supply as well as his own bag of money and his clothes. "I'm glad this is the last trip — I couldn't do this again."

Minnie could only grunt her agreement. She was too weary to answer.

Mr. Haywood had been watching for them, peering over the railing into the darkness. He lowered the ladder when Daisy called and climbed down it carefully.

"Blasted ladder!" he said. "It's hard enough to get up and down in the light, and downright dangerous in the dark. But I'm glad we have it. Someone — sounded like Ducks — was prowling around down here below and talking about what we were up to. What'd you bring? Everything, seems like."

"Only what we'll need," soothed Daisy. "We'll be through hauling soon and then we can all rest."

She moved quickly to tie one bundle at a time to the pulley rope, and Tom scurried up the ladder

161

beside each load to steady it and guide it safely to the deck. Then he sent the rope down for the next one. It was full dark by the time the hens had squawked their frightened way up to the deck of the *Golden Venture*.

"There, there," said Minnie. "Settle down, old girls. You'll be fine by tomorrow. Maybe you can even run around up here."

She stared up at the sky. The masts and rigging loomed over them, and a thin crescent moon climbed the sky. "A new moon," she said. "That's good luck, Addie Tinker always says." For a moment she was terribly homesick. She though of Addie Tinker and the familiar livery stable, and then of her Aunt Addie and their home in St. Joseph. Would it be later now in St. Joe, or earlier? She was too tired to figure it out. All she knew was that the same crescent moon would be shining over Aunt Addie, too, and she wished she was there.

Her homesickness didn't last long. She thought of how shocked Aunt Addie would be to see her, dirty as she was, on the deck of a derelict ship, getting ready to open a store for goldminers. It was a long way from her pleasant sheltered life in St. Joseph, a long way from her blue and white bedroom, a long way from one of Aunt Addie's nourishing, filling suppers in the lamp-lit dining room.

There wasn't much to eat that night, and no time to prepare anything before it was too dark to see. Mr. Haywood opened a box of salt mackerel. It was all he could find.

"Go easy on that fish," he said. "It's salty as all get out. You'll be thirsty all night long." He had found a dipper in the galley and cleaned it as best he could, and the water Tom and Minnie had carted was cool and sweet tasting. It wasn't much of a supper, but to the tired little group it tasted very good. They made sure the ladder and rope were drawn up securely, and opened the lid of the chicken crate. The hens would no doubt choose to stay huddled inside for the night, but by sunup they would be glad to venture out on deck for the corn Minnie scattered.

"They'll be our watch dogs," she said sleepily. "They always squawk if anyone comes around." That was another thing that was very different from St. Joseph. No one there kept watch hens.

Daisy was already straightening the captain's cabin when Minnie stumbled wearily in. "We won't really make up the bed," Daisy said.. "We'll just spread our sheets out over the captain's — whoever he was. That way we won't feel funny about sleeping on a stranger's sheets without washing them. Time enough for that tomorrow."

There was a wash basin on the stand, and Daisy had filled the pitcher with water. They washed swiftly and not very thoroughly by the light of a single candle and were in bed in minutes.

If the ship rocked a little, gently, gently, it only helped to put Minnie to sleep. If rats scurried and squeaked in the hold below, she did not hear. Daisy said, "There's nothing like a sea voyage to make you sleep. Good night, Minnie."

Minnie murmured an answer that was meant to be good night, but she was asleep before she could say the words.

Their first day on the *Golden Venture* was over. There would be many more to come.

15

FOR A MINUTE Minnie didn't know where she was, and then it all came back to her. She sat up in bed, careful not to disturb Daisy, who was still asleep. Yesterday, in their brief trips to the cabin to leave their bundles of blankets and clothing and books, they had had no time for more than a quick look around. And last night it was too dark to do more than fumble for the washbasin in the candlelight. So in the early morning light that came in through the stern window, Minnie looked with interest around the captain's cabin.

It was not a big room, but it didn't have to be large. Every available inch had been fitted with cupboards and drawers and shelves. Beneath the window was a long bench that had two large drawers under the cushioned seat. It would be a good place to stretch out and read or think, and evidently the captain of the *Golden Venture* had done just that. Several books were scattered on the seat, marked with bookmarks.

There was the washstand they had used last night, with a hole cut in the top to hold the basin and pitcher secure, Minnie guessed, if the sea was rough. There was a tall shaving mirror on a stand, something like Pa's, and an elaborate brass lamp hung from the ceiling beams. The bed was built into the wall, and so was the desk where a ledger book was opened. The captain had left his ship in a hurry, not even bothering to put his account books away.

There was still something left in a flat-bottomed decanter on the desk — wine, maybe. Minnie wasn't sure, for Aunt Addie always kept their home-made elderberry wine locked up, to be served in thimble-sized glasses when special visitors came. There was a fancy carpet on the floor, deep rich red with blue and gold figures. It looked elegant and foreign. Perhaps it had come all the way from China. On the wall was a painting of a woman with two children leaning against her knee, looking up at her. Minnie could imagine how the captain had sat at his desk, studying his charts, looking up now and then to see the picture of his wife and children.

She crept out of bed, not making a sound. Daisy stirred in her sleep but did not wake. Let her sleep a little longer, thought Minnie. Daisy had worked like a dog — no, harder than any dog Minnie ever knew — yesterday; and today would be another busy one.

The carpet felt good to her bare feet, the first carpet she had stepped on since she left St. Joe last spring. She stepped up on the bench and peered out of the

high window. The western sky was light now, reflecting all the colors of a bright sunrise. She could see other ships through the low wisps of early morning fog, anchored out beyond in the harbor. Sea gulls flew about, making the strange sounds that were more like a cat's cry than the chirping of birds. She struggled with the window fastening and it squeaked, not a lot of noise but enough to startle Daisy awake.

Daisy sat up quickly and looked around in a daze,

then, just as Minnie had, she remembered where she was and smiled.

"Looks as if we've found a nice little nest for ourselves, doesn't it? I haven't slept so soundly for weeks."

"Oh, Daisy, it's lovely here. Come, look out and see!"

Daisy, still in the petticoat and bodice she had slept in, jumped out of bed and went to the window, too.

"It is nice," she said. "The view's as pretty as it was from up on the hill, only different. But come on, now, we've got to get going. We'll have time to look at the scenery later. Will you look at this dress? I knew I was dirty, but not that dirty! Oh well, things'll dry nicely on the deck this morning, and we each have a clean apron for today, anyway. No, don't put it on now — we'll only be dirty again. Let's wait until we are ready to begin the sale."

Daisy never wasted a minute. She washed with a quick splash of water from the pitcher, dressed in yesterday's wrinkled blue cotton dress, brushed her hair and twisted it up into a knot, all in a few swift motions.

"I'll start our breakfast, whatever that will be," she said as she left the cabin. "I'll have to learn to find my way to our kitchen — it's way up front near the bow, isn't it? I'm all turned around."

Minnie wasn't too far behind her, and as she made her way up the steep stairs to the deck Tom came out of the cabin he shared with Mr. Haywood.

"The mates did themselves proud on this ship,"

he said. "Pretty nice quarters." He was rested and chipper as he scrambled up the stairs behind Minnie. "This sea air has given me an appetite."

"It's the same air you were breathing across the street in the Emporium, and you had a good appetite then, I recall."

"Not like this — watch out for that rope. The crew never should have left things in such disorder. Captain Cavendish wouldn't have stood for it — " He stopped, remembering that even Captain Cavendish had not been able to control his crew once the gold fever took hold of them.

Daisy had the fire going in the stove and was heating water for tea. "We'll have eggs and the rest of this loaf of bread," she said. "Once we get things sorted out, I'll try to do better. If we're to work hard, we must have enough to eat."

Mr. Haywood came up on deck, looking disheveled and still sleepy. He took his mug of tea gratefully and swigged most of it down before he said, "Well, good morning, all. Hope you slept better'n I did. First this old hulk creaked and groaned all night, and then, just as it got light, those gulls began their infernal caterwauling."

"You'll get used to it," said Daisy briskly.

"Don't aim to try," he said. "I'm heading back to Baltimore soon as I help you sell the leftovers and get going here. If I were in my right mind I'd be on my way right now."

"Good thing you aren't," she replied. "We'll need your help. Tom, can you find me a board and something to write with? We'll need a big sign announcing the sale, then we can begin to carry down most of the stuff we hauled up yesterday."

Daisy took it for granted that she would be in charge, and the others were glad to let her take the lead. As soon as their small breakfast was over, she said, "Minnie, you do up these few dishes. We'll have to keep everything extra clean or the rats will move in on us. Tom, bring as much water as you can. Mr. Haywood and I will start to set up the goods for the sale."

They all set to work, and before the rest of the world had started to sir, Daisy had her sign ready. The goods they had salvaged from the ruins of the Emporium were neatly laid out on boards set on barrels.

"It doesn't look like much," said Daisy critically, but Mr. Haywood assured her that it didn't matter, that the miners wouldn't care if the merchandise was smokey. He was right. As soon as passersby saw the sign, "Fire Sale! Big Bargains!" they began to crowd around to buy. Suspenders and harness straps, washbasins and pick axes, all were sold in a few minutes.

"You could charge three times as much and get away with it," Mr. Haywood whispered to Daisy, but she shook her head.

"Fair's fair," she said. "I called it a bargain sale, and it's only honest to give bargains. Yes sir, three cooking pans; here's your change and thank you — No, that was the last of the suspenders — No, there won't be any more. This is a close-out sale. Just pay your money, sir, and never mind the compliments."

Daisy was businesslike and not at all flustered at the admiring remarks the buyers made to her. She ignored their hints and their downright invitations, and only once when one buyer pressed too close did she motion to Minnie to step up with her gun. The miner quietly moved back and faded into the crowd.

Minnie let Mr. Haywood hold her gun for a while while she and Tom sorted in the Emporium wreckage to find more treasures, cloth that was badly charred on the outside but fine when a few yards were unfolded and cut off, small kegs of nails, a hammer or two that needed only new handles. After each find they darted back to Daisy's makeshift counter. She gave each item a quick glance, set a price and sold it almost before it was put down.

"How much for these gloves, Miss Palmer?" someone asked, and Mr. Haywood answered quickly, "Five dollars a pair, fifty dollars for the lot."

"Ridiculous," said Daisy. "Fancy gray kid gloves out here at that price! Two dollars a pair is plenty."

"Then I'll take them all," said Mr. Dan Lawrence. Mr. Haywood groaned. "You'll never make a storekeeper at that rate, Daisy. You'll go broke if you don't listen to me. You've got to charge whatever the traffic will bear."

"He's right, Miss Palmer," said Mr. Lawrence. "You are a babe in the woods at this business. I'm glad you've moved up the street where I can take you

171

under my wing, so to speak. I'm right across the way." He nodded toward his gambling house, The Red Lion, just across the crowded street from the *Golden Venture.*

"You may keep your wing to yourself, Mr. Lawrence, we don't need it. That will be twenty-four dollars for the box, twelve pairs of gloves at two dollars each. Are you aware that they are all different sizes?"

Mr. Haywood groaned again. "Let him find that out, Daisy!"

Mr. Lawrence laughed and then said, "Oh, well, the girls at Emma's place come in all different sizes. They'll like these."

Tom came up then with two left boots. "We can't find the mates, Daisy. Can we sell just one?"

She shook her head, but Mr. Lawrence said, "Nonsense! All you have to do is use a little showmanship." He jumped up on the now almost empty counter and waved the boots.

"Two beautiful left boots!" he shouted. "Waiting for a man with two left feet! Or two men with one sore left foot each. How about it? Who has a left foot that's killing him? Who has a boot that pinches or is cracked? Remember one comfortable foot is better than none at all! Hurry, hurry, they're going fast — Sold to these two gentlemen who are limping, and a bargain at fifteen dollars each!" He handed over the boots, collected the thirty dollars, and hopped down, laughing at Daisy's amazement.

"I can sell song books to canaries, ma'am," he said

confidently. "I think I'll keep an eye on you, Miss Daisy Palmer, whether you like it or not. Maybe you'll be needing a song book." He handed her the money, bowed, and strolled away, making his way through the shoving, pushing crowd. Mr. Haywood gazed after him.

"He's interested in you, Daisy. You could do worse than set your cap for Dan Lawrence."

"Perhaps I could do better, too. A common gambler!"

"Nothing common about him. He's a rich man three times over, they say, and a handsome one, too."

"I haven't time to discuss him," said Daisy, making change out of the roll of bills in her apron pocket. "No, we haven't any hardtack today, sir. The bakery will be going again by tomorrow."

"What is that almost naked Sandwich Islander going to do with a silk cravat when he isn't even wearing a shirt?" Minnie asked Tom as the big brown-skinned man said, "I buy; how much?" Daisy held up one finger, and the dollar and the cravat changed hands. The friend with him immediately bought the remaining one, and they went off together, tying the red flowered silks around their necks.

When every last thing was gone out of the Emporium ashes, except for the food that they didn't want to sell, and the counter was bare, Daisy took down her sign. A protest went up from several who had tried in vain to push through the crowd to buy.

"I'm sorry," she said. "That's all. No, that's all; we have nothing more to sell. Come tomorrow if you want hardtack." Disappointed, the crowd drifted away. When the crush around them was over, Daisy sighed. "That's that," she said in relief. "I dislike being shoved so."

"You'd never guess it," said Mr. Haywood. "Daisy, I'm beginning to think you were born for business. You take to it like a duck to water — "

"Speaking of ducks," said a low voice at her side. "The Sydney Ducks have been taking notice of your little sale." It was Dan Lawrence again. "Lock up tight when you go up to the farm tonight and — "

Daisy turned to him, annoyed. "Mr. Lawrence, if you don't mind, we'll attend to our own safety and you can attend to yours. I thought I'd let you know that we are not interested in being under your wing."

"No offense, Miss Palmer, but you can't stop me from being concerned when I overhear several of the Ducks talking about your prosperity."

Daisy backed down a little. "I'm sorry. We do sincerely thank you for your concern," she said politely, "even if it isn't necessary. But we can take care of the Ducks ourselves. And we aren't living at the farm anymore. We've found a safer abode."

"I'm pleased to hear that. May I ask where?"

She waved her hand at the *Golden Venture* above them.

"We've taken to the sea, Mr. Lawrence. Life aboard a ship suits us just fine."

He was surprised. He pushed his hat back on his head and grinned. "You do beat all, Miss Palmer. Never met another like you. Well, good luck with your sailor's life, but don't blame me if I worry just a little, will you? I'll have some of my men keep an eye out for you."

"It's not necessary," she said again, but this time she was smiling, too. "Come, Tom, Minnie; let's get to work. Mr. Haywood, you take care of the cash box. Good day, Mr. Lawrence."

With as much dignity as if she were leaving a ballroom, Daisy Palmer picked up her full skirt in one hand and started up the rope ladder. Mr. Lawrence stared after her.

"I'll be beat," he said. "I never met another like her."

"And you're not likely to," added Mr. Haywood. "Daisy Palmer's one of a kind." He thought for a moment and then said, "Thank heavens for that. I don't know as the world could cope with two like her."

16

THE NEW BAKERY was a huge success. Minnie thought they had been kept busy in the lean-to of the Emporium, but now they had even more customers. Spring and fine weather and the novelty of a store on an abandoned ship brought more and more people clamoring for hardtack. They worked harder than ever but their working conditions on the *Golden Venture* were so pleasant that the chores did not seem so hard.

For one thing, they had plenty of room up on the deck of the *Golden Venture*. They could move around without knocking each other over. The little shelter they had hastily nailed together was only a skeleton structure, and when they found it was too small they all fell to and took it apart. Tom used the boards for the woodpile, and the new posts that they put up were no more than a support for an old sail. This allowed the breeze to blow through, made pleasant shade when the sun was hot and shielded the bakers and the stoves from the occasional rain.

The worktable was broader and more secure, the shelves where the pieces of hardtack were laid to cool were handier. Daisy set up her supplies in an efficient way to save steps. The stovepipes went straight up in the air so Minnie's time was not spent throwing water on a smoldering wall. Tom carefully removed the sheet of metal under and behind the little galley cookstove and installed it under the stoves on the deck. They felt safe from fire, then, and that was a relief.

Tom kept the three stoves hot and Minnie helped with the mixing and rolling. Mr. Haywood said that for the short time he planned to be there he would tend the store, although he grumbled that it was a crazy kind of store, not like anything he was used to. His job was to stand on the wharf under the sign Daisy had made and take the orders for hardtack. Tom put the thin sheets of bread in a basket he had found, and lowered it by the pulley. The other basket containing the money went up and he emptied it into a box by the railing. The baskets went up and down, up and down all day long. Mr. Haywood kept only enough money in the pocket of his apron to make change when it was necessary.

At the end of each day they counted the money in the box, tallied each one's share and hid it in crocks stored in empty barrels in the unused galley. Tom dumped dried beans over the tops and it would have been very hard to guess that anything but wormy beans was stored there. The piles of coins were growing, but they didn't take time to count what they had earned.

Daisy decided that it was time for a different distribution of the money. "We're all in this together," she said, "so whatever we make will be divided four ways. We're sharing the hardships and we'll share the profits."

When Daisy needed something for the housekeeping she took the money out of the box on the deck and sent Tom and Minnie to a store far up the street.

"It's not like the Emporium," she sighed. "No one else has a fine store like that, Mr. Haywood. But we'll manage."

They discovered that small fish were to be had just for the taking. Tom got up extra early each morning and put a line overboard, and by breakfast time he had a string of delicious small fish for Daisy to fry. The hens had slowed down their laying to just an occasional egg over the winter months. But now they began to lay again and supplied their owners with eggs every day.

For Tom and Minnie the new life aboard the *Golden Venture* was a delight. For Tom it was the next best thing to going to sea, and he taught Minnie the proper nautical name of every rope and mast. The *Golden Venture* was a glorious treasure house for the two young scavengers, although Daisy had forbidden them to go down into the hold. "Rats!" she said, and that was that. But on each expedition to the various cabins, they found useful things to make their quarters more livable. The sofa in one of the passenger cabins was needed on deck now that nice weather had returned. Cushions made of sailors seabags made comfortable seats. The officers' mess below was too close and stuffy, so they moved the table and chairs up on deck to make a pleasant dining room where the breeze from the bay made eating outside an adventure.

Back toward the stern of the boat the hens had

their own fenced-in run, and after a bit of nervous squawking they settled down as if they had always been seafarers.

Mr. Haywood ransacked the galley for a big wash boiler, and strung clotheslines where the sun could quickly dry their clothes. Daisy and Minnie did the wash, but decided to forego ironing. "Except for our aprons," said Daisy. "There's something about me that can't bear a limp, rumpled apron."

Minnie and Daisy discarded their sunbonnets. It was too much to bother with, and both of them liked the sun on their faces. So they turned more golden and tan each day from the warm sun. Minnie had a generous dusting of freckles that would have scandalized Aunt Addie, but after all, Aunt Addie wasn't there to see and scold.

Her letters were there, though. She wrote regularly and the letters came in whenever a ship docked. The Emporium had served as a post office, but now all the letters were delivered to a shack Mr. Lawrence had built onto the Red Lion to be used just for mail distribution. The supply wagons picked up the letters and carried them to the various camps if the address was clear. Seomtimes letters made the rounds of a dozen camps and were finally brought to San Francisco to wait in a pigeonhole for the miner who often never showed up.

The mail for the *Golden Venture* was delivered promptly. Mr. Lawrence saw to it himself, and since he was kind enough to do that, Daisy could hardly be less than civil. He came up the ladder to visit them and was surprised at the comfortable way they had settled into their new quarters.

"You've made a real home of an abandoned ship," he marveled. "It certainly is inviting up here."

Daisy was pleased, and she unbent a trifle and smiled warmly.

"And a place to rest and read, too! Miss Daisy, you are a wonder!" Daisy's cheeks blushed even pinker at the praise, but she went right on rolling hardtack. "The view is very interesting up here," she said.

"What I like best is that you are safer here," he said. "You know I've been troubled about your safety for some time. Here you are sheltered from the rougher elements of our city, and my mind is more at ease."

For once Daisy did not reprove him for being concerned, but said, "Yes, I, too, feel much better about having the children live up here. San Francisco is not an ideal place for impressionable young people," she added, as if his worry had been all about Minnie and Tom.

He always had a good excuse for coming, news from the Stanhopes in Rich Bar, news about the latest ravages of the Sydney Ducks. One day he arrived in his shirt-sleeves bringing a gift wrapped in his fancy tailcoat — a fighting, spitting, half-grown kitten. The instant Mr. Lawrence released her, the cat sprang into the rigging and climbed well above their heads, howling and hissing.

"Oh, dear," he said. "I thought a cat might be a

help in keeping down the rats and mice. I didn't realize she would be a problem."

"A cat is a lovely gift," said Daisy. "She'll settle down, give her time. Here, Tom, set this plate of fish scraps on the deck. She'll be down before long, cozy as can be."

Daisy was both right and wrong. Cozy, as they named the cat, came down eventually, but not until she had called them all every bad name in her cat vocabulary. She scrambled down the rigging about a foot at a time, stopping to hiss if anyone looked at her. Finally she sprang for the food and leaped for the rigging again with the fish tail hanging from her mouth. Minnie was disappointed.

"I'd like to cuddle her," she said. "I haven't played with a kitten since St. Joe."

"Give her time," said Daisy. "She'll make a nice pet yet."

The new bakery was so well run that they were able to make a day's supply of hardtack in much less time and use the rest of their time in other ways. Daisy and Minnie sometimes had time to cook special meals, and Daisy set aside one day a week for making real bread, not the thin hard sheets they sold to the miners. There was often time to relax a little before supper, to read or write or for Minnie and Tom to explore the ship. Daisy read not only the books she had brought in her portmanteau, the ones she had brought to start her school, but those on the captain's shelf as well.

Neither Tom nor Minnie was worried about the

school they were missing, but Daisy felt it was not right. "If you are ever to become a captain, Tom, you'll need to have a firm grasp on figures. Each day you must take some time to practice your sums and calculations. How I wish I understood navigation! I could instruct you in that art. The first mate on the voyage out here to California taught me a little, but not enough to help. He thought I was jesting when I said I wanted to understand it. He couldn't believe a woman meant it."

"I could believe you meant it," said Mr. Lawrence to Daisy. He often stopped by in the late afternoon to sit in the shade of the sail canopy and visit with her as she read or sewed. On this day he had brought a letter from Aunt Addie to Minnie. "Now that I am better acquainted with you, I can believe you are capable of doing anything in the world."

Daisy blushed and turned the conversation to Minnie's letter. "What does your aunt say, Minnie? I hope the news from St. Joseph is good."

"Things seem to be fine, Daisy. Aunt Addie has hardly anything to complain about. She makes poor Addie Tinker follow all her orders, and the livery stable is thriving, she says. I guess Pa'll have his hands full when he gets back — Aunt Addie will still want to run things. Banker Hanlon advises her on every step, she says, and she has bought three more horses and a new buggy just for hiring out. She's still scolding about our leaving, though. I wish she wouldn't worry. Listen to this —

" 'Minnie, I cannot bear to think what your poor

dear little mother would say about your present venture. It disturbs me to think of you working as a baker's helper, of all things, in such a wild settlement. I only hope that the experience is not too coarsening, and that you will be able to resume your life as the well brought up young girl I have always wished for. I pray that you will come through this trial safely and that it will soon be only a horrible memory. Try not to be influenced by your rough companions, and, if you can, be a good influence on them.'"

Minnie stopped reading to giggle. "Am I a good influence, Daisy? She says, 'Pierce, wherever you are, I am sure your soul must be in torment when you think of the dangers to which you have exposed that gentle child.'"

Daisy smiled. "Your Aunt Addie would be surprised to see you now," she said. "Your work over for the day, resting in the shade, reading a book. I don't think this is what she imagines it to be."

"Rough companions!" said Mr. Lawrence indignantly. "There's no lady in San Francisco who can compare to you, Miss Palmer!"

Daisy smiled broadly. "That's not much of a compliment, Mr. Lawrence," she said. "There are mighty few women in San Francisco, and even fewer ladies. Perhaps you might say I win by default. Oh, gracious, look at the sunset — it's way past time to prepare supper. Good day, Mr. Lawrence, and thank you for bringing the mail, though I assure you, Tom or Mr. Haywood would be glad to call for it."

After Mr. Lawrence had gone down the ladder, Mr. Haywood said, "You've got a mighty good friend in Dan Lawrence, Daisy. A girl like you, all alone in the world, shouldn't be so choosy. Who knows when someone as rich as that will come along again?"

Daisy only said, "Money isn't everything. Minnie, will you peel enough potatoes for our supper while I fix the stew?"

"Money isn't everything," he insisted, "but having no money isn't *anything!* It's your good I'm thinking of, Daisy."

Daisy changed the subject to something else.

Letters from Minnie's father were few and far between. He had a hard time finding any kind of paper to write on, and an even harder time finding a miner who was going back into San Francisco. Now that the winter was over the traffic was mostly one way, toward the gold fields.

Finally he found that if he drove into Hangtown proper (he said that Hangtown proper was a joke; there was nothing at all proper about Hangtown) from the outskirts where he was prospecting, he could send his letters out by the supply wagons. He wrote that he was panning steadily, and that while his finds were not sensational, his poke was growing heavier each day with flakes and dust and small nuggets of gold.

He skimmed over any problems he might be having and only said that he was ever watchful of his poke and tools and team. But Mr. Lawrence reported that thievery and brawls were on the increase in all the camps as more and more gold-hungry men surged into the gold fields.

"Then how can you justify coaxing Mrs. Stanhope and her daughters to Rich Bar?" cried Daisy indignantly when Mr. Lawrence brought this piece of news.

"I promised them they'd be safe, and they are," he said. "They are living comfortably and safely in Rich Bar's only hotel, and they're looking after Mr. Stanhope's welfare. He's getting better every day, and the girls are much looked up to and respected. Men drive twenty miles to hear them sing and play, and they've become famous."

"Humph!" was all Daisy would say to that. Mr. Lawrence had no specific news from Hangtown for Minnie, but he promised that he would inquire about Pierce Weldon from any miners who came in from there.

"I doubt very much if Mr. Weldon's kind of friends would be coming to a place like the Red Lion," declared Daisy. Minnie agreed, but she hoped Mr. Lawrence would ask anyway. Letters were fine, but she wished she could hear directly from someone who had actually seen her father and talked to him.

Then came a spell with no letters at all. Six weeks went by without a word from her father. At first Minnie wasn't too worried, but as the days went by without a letter she felt more and more lonely and lost. She tried not to show it as it would only distress the others and could do no good.

What if something awful happened to her father in that dreadful place? Captain Cavendish had been away almost as long, but Tom had received only a few short notes. He wasn't alarmed at all and said that was how sea captains were. So Minnie did her best to appear unconcerned. It wasn't easy. She fooled Tom and Mr. Haywood, but Daisy saw through her pretenses.

"You aren't eating, Minnie, and you aren't sleeping well, either. Tomorrow I'm going to ask Mr. Lawrence if he'll make a special effort to get some news of your father. It's worth trying, don't you think?"

Just the idea was a comfort and that night Minnie tossed less in her sleep. When she awoke, though, the worry was still heavy as a stone in her chest and she had to swallow hard to get her breakfast down.

The bakery was open for the day and business was brisk as usual. Minnie had gone to get more flour from the storeroom, and when she came up on deck she heard a commotion on the wharf below.

"Oh, no you don't, Mister! Nobody goes up that ladder without my say-so!" That was Mr. Haywood. The man said something and Mr. Haywood answered, "A likely story!" There were laughs and jeers from the crowd of buyers, and then Mr. Haywood called, "Tom, hit the bum when he gets to the top!" Tom hurried to the railing with a heavy skillet in his hand, and Minnie grabbed up her gun and raced after him. Daisy gasped, "The Ducks!"

A ragged man with a bush of brown beard was coming slowly up the ladder, and just as Tom raised his skillet, the man looked up and shouted, "Minnie!"

It was her father. She didn't recognize the gaunt face, but there was no mistaking the voice. It was really her father.

17

THE CLIMB to the deck of the *Golden Venture* had used all of Pierce Weldon's strength. Daisy and Tom supported him and Minnie ran to spread cushions in the shade of their sail awning. His legs buckled and he sat down with a thump.

"Feels so good — " he mumbled. "I'm all right, just a touch of fever left — sick so long — had to hold on until I found my Minnie — "

"Lie down," said Daisy gently. He lay down obediently and closed his eyes. Minnie whispered fearfully, "Is he — ?"

"Not at all. He's just worn out, I think." Daisy felt his forehead. "A little fever. Tom, will you bring water and a towel, and Minnie, will you fetch a sheet? He mustn't get chilled, even though the sun is warm."

When Minnie hurried up again to the deck, Daisy was dipping a towel in the cool water and sponging her patient's face and wrists. "We'll let him sleep as long as he wants and by the time he wakens we'll have some nourishing food for him."

Mr. Haywood was calling from below, impatient to know what was going on. Daisy called down to him, "We burned that last batch of hardtack, Mr. Haywood. Tell all our customers that we're closing early today. We'll open up again tomorrow morning. Come up, we have a surprise for you."

Mr. Haywood tried to appease several annoyed customers who were disappointed to hear this. "I don't know what's goin' on, no more'n you do!" he said. "Daisy," he yelled, "you can't run a business like this! You've got all these folks waitin' to spend their money. If you send 'em off, they'll only drink or gamble it away!"

"Then they're fools," she called cheerfully. "Sorry, gentlemen, the hardtack will be fresher and crisper the first thing tomorrow morning. I promise we'll have an extra lot on hand for you. Come back tomorrow." She waved them away, and after grumbling a little, the group of miners broke up and drifted away.

Mr. Haywood toiled up the ladder, complaining as he always did. "Why I was fool enough to say I'd stay and help you, I'll never know. I could be almost home by now."

"You could be hanging over a rail now, seasick and miserable. At least on the *Golden Venture* you never get seasick. Hush, Minnie's father is sleeping."

"Minnie's father? Well, I'm glad you saw fit to tell me. Is he sick? Or drunk — "

190

"Ssh! He's been very sick, I think, and he's still got a fever. We'll let him rest and we'll feed him properly. He'll be much better soon."

Minnie sat by her father's side all afternoon, bathing his flushed face occasionally, watching that the awning shaded him as the sun swung around to the west. Daisy went below to open and air the cabin next to the one Tom and Mr. Haywood shared. She dusted the little room and spread fresh sheets and a blanket. Daisy had long ago opened the chests and lockers and washed the bedding that would soon have mildewed. The ocean breeze came in through the porthole, and very soon Mr. Weldon's cabin was ready.

Never wasting a minute, she was soon back on deck preparing supper for them all. She cooked up a nourishing broth for Minnie's father and set it on the back of the stove to simmer until he wakened. Minnie got up to help, but Daisy shook her head and motioned Minnie back to her father's side.

"Stay there," Daisy whispered. "You should be right there when he wakens. I'll bring your supper to you."

Pierce Weldon slept on, through supper and sunset, while bright stars sparkled in the sky through the early evening hours. Finally it was late and still he hadn't wakened.

"He's probably too weak to make those steep stairs, anyway. Tom, let's get the mattress from his cabin," suggested Mr. Haywood. "Then Minnie can get some sleep and still be here when he wakes up.

Wouldn't do for a sick man to wake up and find himself all alone on the deck of a strange ship."

Daisy nodded, and in a short time Tom and Mr. Haywood were struggling up the steep stairs with the mattress and a blanket and a pillow. Minnie protested that she wouldn't be able to sleep a wink, that she didn't want to lie down, that she was perfectly comfortable, but Daisy would stand for no argument. She made up Minnie's pallet by her father's side, left a clean towel and a basin of water close by, and said good night in a whisper.

Minnie soon found she was sleepier than she had thought. She listened for a moment to her father's deep steady breathing, and before she knew it she was sound asleep, too. She never knew another thing until the morning sun fell on her face.

She came to the surface of wakefulness slowly, trying to sort out why she was sleeping in the open, wrapped in a blanket against the chill morning breeze. She stared at the mast and rigging rising above her and decided she was dreaming, when Cozy jumped on her and licked her face. She really woke then and knew it was real, and not a confusing dream. Her father was still sleeping, she thought. She turned over to find that she was wrong. His eyes were open and he was gazing about him in confused wonder.

"Pa!"

"Minnie, sprat, is it really you?"

It took more than a moment to convince him that he too was wide awake and clear in his mind, not

192

muddled with fever. "Are we out to sea, lovey?"

"No, no, we're on a ship, but she's anchored at the wharf here. Don't you worry; we've got a good safe place here, and we'll feed you and take care of you until you're well and strong again."

He sank back on the cushions, exhausted by the effort of sitting up and looking around. "Dang it all, Minnie, I'm weak as a cat. Don't have the strength of a little baby. So sick — so long — but I had to get back to find you — " His voice trailed off and he closed his eyes.

Minnie jumped up, saying, "You mustn't try to talk. Just lie still and rest, and let us all take care of you. I'll heat the broth — that'll make you stronger."

She tried to be quiet as she raked down the ashes in one of the stoves and poked up the handful of embers that were still glowing. She was careful not to bang the stove lids or make a lot of noise as she put in the firewood, but as quiet as she tried to be, Daisy heard. She came hurrying up the stairs, running across the deck, fastening the neck of her dress as she ran.

"Is your father all right, Minnie?" she asked urgently in a low voice, and Minnie was glad to be able to answer that he seemed much better, but very weak.

The fire blazed up and the pot of broth was soon warm. "I think maybe we should try just thin broth first," worried Daisy. "That can't hurt him any. Later, if he can eat it, we'll thicken it up and make it richer. If only I knew more about nursing." She

lifted his head gently and had Minnie shove pillows under his back so that he could sit up enough to eat. He opened his eyes to stare at her in amazement, and Minnie remembered then that he had never met Daisy at all. Not Daisy, nor Tom, and Mr. Haywood only in passing. When Pa left her she was in the care of Mrs. Stanhope. No wonder he looked confused.

"It's all right, Pa. Have a sip of broth — careful, now — and when you are stronger we'll explain it all. There, isn't that good? Another spoonful, just one more."

When he finally closed his eyes again, too weary to hold them open any longer, he was smiling a little, and he had managed to finish half a bowl of soup.

"Good!" Daisy was pleased. "A little more each time he wakens, and we'll have your father well again in no time. Now please eat some breakfast, Minnie, love. You must be starved. You hardly ate enough to keep a bird alive last night."

Minnie admitted that she did feel hollow all the way to her toes. And when Daisy had made her a hearty breakfast of fried mush and bacon, she made short work of it.

Tom and Mr. Haywood were up by then. Tom flung his fishing lines over the rail and soon had a catch of small silver fish. Cozy got the heads and tails and the rest went into Daisy's frying pan. Minnie was still hungry enough to polish off her share of fish, but she did not sit up at the table with the others. She took her plate and sat at her father's side, ready to answer if he spoke.

The waterfront street noises seemed far away. Down on the wharf, in an effort to be quiet, Mr. Haywood modified his customary bellow to an occasional shout. Once in a while if business slackened a little he would call out, "You, there! Need any fresh delicious hardtack?" But at the end of the afternoon he marveled.

"We did as well or better'n any other day, and I hardly raised my voice. What d'you know? I got

195

strength enough left to do it all over again."

Up on deck, Daisy and Tom moved around as busily as ever, but with a special effort to be quiet. Tom moved the hen's crate way to the stern of the *Golden Venture* so even their soft contented clucking would not disturb Pierce Weldon's rest. Cozy was shut in Tom's cabin to keep her out of mischief. Minnie helped with the day's baking, but with an eye always on her father. As soon as he stirred, they propped him up on pillows and urged him to try a little more soup.

Once when he sniffed appreciatively at the fragrance of baking hardtack, they soaked a crisp sheet of it in his broth and fed it to him bite by bite.

Late in the afternoon Mr. Lawrence climbed up the rope ladder with some letters, one for Tom and one for Daisy from the Stanhopes.

"I wish I had one for Minnie," he apologized to Daisy. "The news from Hangtown isn't good. Cholera broke out last month and the men've been dying like flies up there, I hear. Don't tell the little girl. I know she's worried about her father."

Daisy's smile was radiant. "Not any more, she isn't. There he is now, sound asleep. He's been very sick, that's plain, but he's on the mend. We'll pull him through."

"I'm sure you will, Miss Daisy."

When Minnie saw Mr. Lawrence she hurried over to share the good news. The gambler said, as if he really meant it, "I'm so glad, Minnie. He'll be fine with two good nurses —"

"Four," said Minnie. "Tom and Mr. Haywood are taking their turns, too."

"Four, then," said Mr. Lawrence. "Four people who care about him. He's a very lucky man."

18

PIERCE WELDON'S RECOVERY was not immediate,
but it was steady. Each day he ate a little more
and needed a little less sleep. His voice grew
stronger and he was able to sit up in a chair. He tried
to walk, but his legs were still too unsteady to go it
alone. Every morning before the bakery opened,
Tom and Mr. Haywood walked him a short distance
up and down the deck, and each day he was able to
walk better.

Long before he was able to manage by himself they
had all done a lot of talking and explaining. He had
to know about the Stanhopes and get acquainted with
other members of Minnie's new family. Fortunately he liked them as well as Minnie did, and the strange-
ness they all felt at the beginning soon was gone. He
fished with Tom over the rail and told the boy stories
of his fishing in the Missouri River. Mr. Haywood
even found him a patient listener to all his complaints
and worries.

When he was well enough to sit up and talk about it,

Minnie's father told them about his life in the mining camp near Hangtown.

"It was pretty dreary," he said. "I got lonesome for someone to talk to, but I soon found it was a lot safer to keep to myself and be lonely rather than to run the risk of falling in with thieves just for the sake of company. Oh, the men in the fields are mostly good fellows, but it takes only a few bad ones to make trouble, and let me tell you there were more than a few bad ones. I learned never to let my animals or wagon out of my sight, and I wore my poke tied around my waist until it got so heavy I fell over when I tried to crouch down to pan." He stopped to laugh at the memory of how he had unexpectedly tipped over in the ice-cold mountain stream.

"So then I made a false bottom under the wagon seat and hid my gold there — and lost the whole business when those thugs stole my wagon. Maybe they'll never find my poke and get any good out of it, but it doesn't matter, neither will I. Back when I first knew I was getting sick I thought I could treat myself and get over it, but then I kept fainting and I got light in my head and began to talk to myself, crazy stuff. So then I packed up as best I could and tried to drive into Hangtown, hoping I might find a doctor, maybe. But I never quite made it. That was when someone hit me on the head — never saw who it was. All I knew was that I came to after a while with a lump on my head big as a goose egg, and the wagon and mules and poke were gone. I managed to ask the driver of one of the supply wagons for a ride into San Francisco. After I fell off the seat once or twice, he bundled me into the back of the wagon. I passed out, don't even remember the trip in, except that I knew everything was gone, all gone. Not a thing to show for all those months of hard work. So there it is, Minnie. Your Aunt Addie was right — she said I'd lose everything and I did. We're stone broke, lovey. We've got less than we started out with. Poor as church mice, and no chance of buying our freedom now."

He shook his head sadly. "All gone, all gone, and now my health's gone, to boot."

Daisy leaned over to pat his hand reassuringly. "Now, there," she said. "Your health, at least, is coming back. You're much stronger today than yesterday. You mustn't despair, Mr. Weldon."

Mr. Haywood blew his nose loudly. "I know just how you feel, only I was lucky enough to hang on to my savings, thank goodness. Don't give up, man, things'll get better."

Tom asked, "What do you mean, Mr. Weldon, 'buy your freedom'? Aren't you free already?"

Mr. Weldon shook his head. "That's the worst of it. That's what this whole trip west was all about, to buy our freedom from Minnie's Aunt Addie. Oh," he added, "I'm not saying Miss Addie meant to hold us in bondage — no, not that! A kinder woman never lived, but — kind in her own peculiar way, I guess. I wanted to be able to go home with a bag of gold big enough to build a new house with, to let us get out of her debt and live our own lives, Minnie and I. Now I don't even have a mule or a wagon to get us home in."

Minnie swallowed hard. She remembered the excitement of the trip west, of the times when she and Pa had ridden along side by side on the wagon seat, planning for their future. They had such high hopes, and now —

Then she remembered the coins in the crocks, hidden away in the storeroom next to the ship's galley. She was up and off in an instant. The others stared as she raced across the deck to the hatch leading below. She was soon back again, lugging one of the heavy crocks.

"There!" she panted, setting it down with a thump. "This is only one of them. It's my share of the bakery. Maybe there's enough here to buy our freedom anyway." He watched open mouthed as she tipped over the crock and a stream of coins and nuggets spilled out on the deck.

Tom jumped up to step on the coins that spun away, and then they all crowded around as Daisy began to count it. "We've been too busy to stop and count," she said. "I didn't realize our business had been so good. One, two, three," she began to stack the coins in neat piles beside Mr. Weldon's cot. She heaped the nuggets and the little packets of gold dust to one side. "Tom, get your notebook and help me tally," she said excitedly. "I'll lose track!"

Pa said, "Wait a minute. If this is Minnie's money, I'm not about to use it to get me out of my foolishness."

Minnie shook her head. "It's my freedom, too, Pa. It's for both of us."

Mr. Haywood was helping to count now, too. "Mr. Weldon, there's enough here for just about anything you need. Your little girl has been a real moneymaker, thanks to Daisy's business head and her own hard work. Of course she could've made a lot more, a whole lot more, if she'd been willing to skin people a trifle." He shook his head as if regretting all the chances Minnie had wasted. "They drove a close bargain, she'n Daisy did, but always a fair one. I'll attest to that, sir."

Pa didn't know what to say. "How — how — " he asked.

So Minnie started back at the very beginning when she and the Stanhopes had first met Miss Daisy Palmer in the Emporium. She told how the hardtack business had begun, and then the laundry, and then how Tom had happened to join them. Then she told about the fire in the Emporium and the constant danger from the Sydney Ducks. She even told about the time she and Tom had bested the Ducks and brought back the rabbit. That was a surprise for Daisy and Mr. Haywood. Daisy said sternly, "Minnie, that was *very* dangerous! You must never take a chance like that again — " she stopped, flustered and blushing.

"I'm so sorry, Mr. Weldon. I didn't mean to be so bossy. I forgot that Minnie is your responsibility now — just force of habit — "

"Don't be sorry, Miss Daisy. You are right to keep

an eye on this little girl. She's headstrong, as you know, or she wouldn't be out here at all. She needs a good woman to guide her — " He stopped, too. There was an embarrassed pause, and then Mr. Haywood said, "Neither of them kids is perfect. They both need a firm hand, but they're good children. Not too many like them around."

"There will be more. More children coming in to San Francisco every day," said Daisy. She sounded glad to change the subject. "Last year all the new arrivals were men, but this year there are a few families, I notice. Families planning to stay and settle, I hope. This will be a good influence on this wild town."

"Maybe they'll need a school, Daisy!" Tom explained to Mr. Weldon. "Daisy's a schoolteacher and she's saving her money to start a new kind of school, one where it'll be interesting to learn. And she can do it, too. She can make anything interesting."

Daisy blushed again. "Time to start our supper, Minnie. Tom, we'll need firewood."

They had talked about the Sydney Ducks as if that danger was in the past. They felt secure in their shipboard roost and slept soundly at night. But they knew that the Ducks were still running riot in the city. Often the flames of burning buildings lighted up the sky, and more often than not they heard shouting and fighting down below on the waterfront street. It would take more than the arrival of a few families to make the city safe.

203

They talked about it more than once in the late afternoons after the bakery had closed for the day. "It's a beautiful place," Pa often said thoughtfully. "A person couldn't ask for a prettier sight than that sunset, now, and the green on the hills running down to the water."

"The light on those flimsy buildings makes them look as if they were made of pure gold," added Daisy.

"The climate's pure gold most of the time," Mr. Haywood offered. "Makes me wonder if I'm out of my head to be goin' back to Baltimore. Hot in the summer, cold in the winter — makes me wonder."

It was one day when Pa was still wobbly in his legs that the Stanhopes came back to town. Minnie and Tom had each taken two pails to bring back a supply of fresh water. Pa said nervously, "I wish I could go with them," but Daisy answered confidently, "Now, don't you worry. They can manage fine by themselves. San Franciscans, even the roughest ones, have learned to have a lot of respect for Minnie and her gun; and Tom's ready with his fists. Don't worry."

Minnie always welcomed the chance to get off the *Golden Venture* once in a while for a change of scene. As pleasant as life was aboard ship, she did like to see what was going on down at street level. There were always new people arriving in outlandish costumes, the like of which she had never seen before. And the antics of the excited newcomers who were sure they were on the road to fabulous riches! They poured down the waterfront street, stopping to bargain at the rickety stalls and shops in all sorts of languages and dialects.

She and Tom had filled their pails at the well behind the rubble that had been the Emporium and had started back up the street to the ship when they heard a shout.

"Ho, there, Minnie! Tom! Whoa, Brownie! Whoa, there! Girls, it's Minnie and Tom!"

It was the Stanhopes. Ruby and Pearl were standing up in the back of the wagon waving parasols. Mrs. Stanhope was driving, flourishing a long whip that never touched Brownie, but whistled alarmingly close to the heads of any passersby who ventured to call out to the girls. On the seat beside her was a smiling little man, not a bit taller than Mrs. Stanhope.

"Josephus!" she was yelling. "It's my children, there they are!" He smiled and waved and Mrs. Stanhope turned the wagon around with a grind of the wheels and brought it up beside Minnie and Tom with a squeaking flourish.

There was general hugging and laughing, asking of questions, answers. In the hubbub they gathered that the Stanhopes had gone up to the farmhouse and found it deserted, with Daisy's note too faded and discolored to read. They were on their way now to Mr. Lawrence's gambling house to ask where Daisy and the children might have gone.

"I was prepared to tear him apart if he'd let anything happen to you all," she said. "We're quitting his Opera House, and I've got to break the news to him — but where's Daisy? And the Emporium, what happened? Where are you living? Hop on the wagon and let's go!"

They scrambled over the tail gate of the wagon, stopping an instant to pat the brown cow who was still patiently following behind, and directed Mrs. Stanhope to the ship just up the street. In a moment they had pulled up in front of the *Golden Venture*.

There was more shouting as they spied Mr. Haywood and his hardtack stand, and even more as they climbed up the ladder to the deck. Tom elected to sit on the rail where he could keep one eye on the horse and wagon, for it was piled with all the Stanhope belongings. It would have been a likely target for the thieves who operated boldly in broad daylight. From the railing he could watch the wagon and yet not miss a word of the excited conversation.

Minnie had hurried up the ladder first to show them how, and she and Daisy stood at the railing encouraging the Stanhopes' shakey progress.

"It jiggles, but it's perfectly safe — that's it, one step at a time," called Daisy. Minnie whispered to her, "That's Mr. Josephus Stanhope. I thought he'd be at least nine feet tall, the way Mrs. Stanhope talked."

"The eye of love," answered Daisy. "She loves him, so he *is* nine feet tall, however short he looks to us."

Then there was another happy reunion on the deck, with more shouting and hugging. To questions about the Opera House, Mrs. Stanhope declared,

206

"It was an experience, but it's over. It was interesting while it lasted, and funny sometimes, and a couple of times it was scarey. I must say the fame and fortune didn't spoil our girls one bit, not with me and Josephus there to keep their heads on straight. But it's all over. We've found a nice piece of land between the Sacramento and the Feather River, not a goldminer within miles and no chance of a gold strike there; it's not the right kind of territory, praise the Lord! So we're back to farming again. We can have a house of sorts built by the rainy season and in the spring we'll plant. We've got Bossie as the start of our herd, and in no time we'll be settled in."

They stayed for a meal that Daisy served picnic style in the sunshine, full of talk of their new home, of the possibility that other families would join them in the area.

"As long as this gold madness lasts, and long after," said Mr. Josephus Stanhope, "folks'll be needing food and a decent kind of civilization, and we aim to be part of it. Good God-fearing husbands for our girls, a church, a school — we'll have 'em all afore long. Most of these miners'll get discouraged and leave, but not all. Some will settle. Mark my words, in times to come this Californy land'll be like the Promised Land."

Soon the Stanhopes were off to break the news to Dan Lawrence that the stars of his Opera House were returning to a farm. They left, promising to write, and shouting directions to the farm as they drove over to the Red Lion.

The Stanhope visit had affected them all. Minnie and Tom laughed about the funny stories the family had to tell about life in Rich Bar at the elegant Palace Hotel — with the pen of chickens brought in each night for safety, and the stretched calico walls that were the only partitions between rooms.

Daisy and Pa and Mr. Haywood didn't laugh. They were subdued and thoughtful. But none of them volunteered to say where their thoughts were taking them.

19

P<small>A GREW STRONGER</small> each day, and before long he was taking on his own share of chores on the ship. He and Tom cut firewood to keep the stoves going. They rowed out to some of the nearby ships, ships that had been abandoned to the wind and weather and rats. If it was clear that the ship was beyond all repair, they chopped down rotting spars and masts and cut them into lengths to fit the stoves.

Pa stoked the fires and took the finished hardtack off the stoves with long tongs. As soon as it was cool enough, Tom tied it up in small bundles and sent it down on the pulley for Mr. Haywood's impatient customers.

With three stoves going full blast, Daisy said it was a shame to use only the stove tops and let all that good oven space go to waste. So each evening she set a huge pan of yeast bread to rise and early every morning she and Minnie punched and kneaded and shaped it into loaves.

The wonderful smell of baking bread was borne landward by the breeze from the bay, and even over the really terrible odors of rotting bilge and dust and horse manure and none-too-clean bodies, people knew that something very good was baking. In no time at all customers learned that if they wanted the treat of good fresh bread they had to be in line early. The crowds started to gather not long after daylight, and more coins than ever jingled in the basket. The new hotel that Mr. Lawrence had built across the street next to the Red Lion was full to overflowing all the time, and he ordered as much bread each day as they could let him have.

The little group on the *Golden Venture* was working harder than ever, but it was happy hard work. They enjoyed the labor, and even more they enjoyed the precious bit of leisure they snatched each day after their work was over. When supper was finished they lingered on the deck until it was dark, talking and laughing, discussing things until finally Daisy said they must get some rest to be ready for the next day.

Pa and Daisy did most of the discussing, and the others leaned back against the comfortable sea-bag cushions and listened. It was fun to hear them disagree, to hear the spirited arguments, the sparks flying as they took different sides to a question. It was the first time Pa had had someone to talk books with, as far as Minnie could remember, and he seemed to be enjoying it enormously.

Once Minnie thought, "It's too bad Pa's set his

heart on finding a sweet gentle person like my mama was. Daisy is so — so special."

One evening they began to talk of plans for the time when San Francisco would settle down to normal growth, when the gold madness was over, and there would be a settled population needing more than fly-by-night services.

Daisy was the first one to come out with her ideas. "I've been thinking," she said one evening as they rested and enjoyed the sunset. "I'm not going to be content to run a bakery always. I haven't for one moment given up my plan to start a small school. There is work to be done in education, much needed work, and I want to do it. For so long I was planning to work here just long enough to make my passage back to Boston and begin there. But lately, it seems that I can't bear to leave this wonderful country, and surely a school is needed more out here than back home in the East. My family is gone and I have few ties there, so California is where I want to settle."

She reached for another shirt to mend. Daisy seldom sat down without some sort of handwork to occupy her, and her frugal New England nature would not let her throw away any garment that could be rescued. Minnie had her own workbasket. She kept her father's clothes in repair, as well as her own.

From time to time the thought had occured to Minnie that this contented period was not a permanent one, that the time would come when they would separate and go their own ways. Every time the thought popped up Minnie pushed it right back down. She didn't want to think about it.

Now when Daisy spoke as if her mind were really made up, Minnie felt a pang inside, a feeling of loss. Her eyes suddenly brimmed with tears and she bent over her mending so that no one else would notice. Pa stopped a moment in his whittling and looked at Daisy, and then went on working again.

Mr. Haywood laughed his dry cackling laugh. "Bless my soul, Daisy, we've been thinking along the same lines. I've been saying over and over to myself, why make that long hard trip back to Baltimore? My friends — the few I had years ago — have scattered, and I'd be on my own, hot in the summer, freezing in the winter. Why do it? I've decided I'm for Californy too, and what's more I'm going to start a business again. I'm a storekeeper right through to my bones, that's certain, and I don't think I could be happy just settin' around. I've given it a lot of thought and that's what I want to do."

"It'd be hard to find a more likely spot than San Francisco," Pa said thoughtfully. "If we didn't have responsibilities in St. Joe — "

Minnie's heart had leaped up for a second and then it sank. Of course, she and Pa would have to go back to St. Joseph. His livery stable was there, and they couldn't leave Aunt Addie stranded alone in a town she had never really liked. Of course they would have to go back. She snuffled hard and got her tears under control. For just an instant it had been a lovely dream.

Tom looked up from his book of navigation. "I'm going back to sea just as soon as Captain Cavendish sails again, but I'll come to see you, Daisy and Mr. Haywood, every time we get into port here."

That made it worse. Tom'd never get so far inland as Missouri, never. She wiped her nose quickly on her sewing and thought, as she did it, "Aunt Addie'll never stand for that. I'll have to start mending my ways."

She had a lot to think about that night, and for a long time sleep refused to come. Daisy slept soundly, but Minnie tossed and turned and punched her pillow to make it more comfortable. At last she dozed off. When she woke again the pink light of sunrise was coming in through the high stern windows. Daylight so early! She felt as if she had hardly gone to sleep. She tried to close her eyes and get just a bit more rest before their busy day began.

"Wait a minute!" she said to herself, suddenly wide awake. "That window faces west — it can't be the sunrise!"

She was out of bed and standing on the bench in a flash. The sky was pink, all right, but it was not from the sun! The waterfront was on fire. The ship next to the *Golden Venture* had not yet caught, but beyond that a small brig was blazing away with flames crackling fiercely up the mast. Sparks flew everywhere, and the deck of the *Orpheus* next door was beginning to smolder.

It couldn't have been more than a few seconds that Minnie stood frozen there. Then she screamed, a piercing scream that brought Daisy upright and woke Tom in the next cabin.

"Get Pa up," she shouted. "Wake Mr. Haywood!" Then she saw something that was more frightening than the fire. On the deck of the *Orpheus* she could see black figures silhouetted against the flames, men who were deliberately spreading the fire.

"The Ducks!" she gasped. "They've come to get us!"

She and Daisy threw their dresses on over their nightgowns and raced up the stairs with Tom and Pa and Mr. Haywood pounding behind them.

"They're planning to loot!" Mr. Haywood said. "Let's get off this death trap fast as we can." Without question they all turned toward the bow and ran for the ladder. Suddenly Minnie thought, "We can't leave the hens here to burn, and Cozy — well, she can scramble down — but all that money we've worked so hard to earn — Daisy's school and Mr. Haywood's store and — No! Not to those Ducks!"

"No!" she yelled, quite forgetting to be afraid, "I'm going to get my gun!"

Mr. Haywood grabbed her skirt and held on. "Minnie, you can't hold off the Ducks, and the fire'll get us even if you could! Pierce, make her hurry!"

But the momentary pause had given Pierce Weldon time to get his wits together too. "Minnie's right," he said. "The Ducks aren't going to get all you worked so hard for. Minnie, go get your gun, you know how to find it quickest, and we're not on fire yet. Then you and Tom and Daisy go down the ladder. Go to a safe place and wait. Go to Dan Lawrence's. Mr. Haywood, we'll save the money — "

Daisy said, "Oh, no you don't! Don't you dare send me away like a child! It's my home and my money, too. I can fight off the Ducks — "

"Daisy, darling, you and Tom and Minnie get down that ladder and run!" Pa shouted. "Don't be so pigheaded!"

"Not me," said Tom. "No siree, Mr. Weldon! Minnie and I can hold our own right here. There are fire buckets around. Minnie and I can fill them."

All this took only another minute or two, and once Pierce Weldon saw that no one intended to obey him and run, he gave up. "All right then, we'll work together. Mr. Haywood, Miss Daisy, get the crocks. We'll load things in the dinghy. Get the gun, Minnie. Tom, go down into the dinghy, hurry!"

When the stoneware crocks and the hen coop were all passed down to Tom and loaded in, there was still plenty of room. Daisy ran to get armloads of her books. Minnie bundled all their dishes into a tablecloth and dumped it in. They piled in a keg of flour, a side of bacon — everything they could lay hands on in a hurry. Then the boat was loaded; Tom took the oars and rowed vigorously into the darkness away from the *Golden Venture.*

Pa stationed himself by the rail with Minnie's gun ready. Daisy and Minnie and Mr. Haywood were ranged along the rail, each with a fire bucket and a heavy belaying pin at hand. They crouched below the rail, and if the rampaging Ducks could have seen through the glare and smoke they would have guessed that the occupants of the *Golden Venture* had fled or were huddled below, terrified.

One torch of burning rags was flung onto the wet deck and sizzled itself out. A Duck was heard to shout, "You idiots! Don't set that one afire until we've found the stuff! You stupid clinker, you'll do us outta the money!"

"I want the money, and I want that black-haired girl!" another shouted drunkenly, and Minnie could feel Daisy shudder. "I'll give him a Black-Haired Girl that he won't forget," she muttered.

There were shouts from the street now, unmistakably Duck voices, so that way of escape was cut off. "Hurry up, Joe, toss the stuff down!" someone called impatiently. "They're still up there, no one has gotten off!"

Minnie was glad they hadn't lowered the ladder. There was quite a space between the *Orpheus* and the *Golden Venture*, but not so much that a strong man couldn't leap across. The first of the dark figures got a running start across the deck, and the defenders of the *Venture* tightened their muscles and got ready. Still crouched down, they could hear his feet pounding on the deck, and the hoarse shouts of encouragement from his friends. A moment's awful suspense, and then a wild splash! He had missed. There was swearing and shouting and someone said, "Get a plank — we can walk across!" but another voice, less drunk than the rest said, "Wait, I can swing over on this rope!"

Whoever he was, he was strong, for he came swinging over their heads in a wide arc, but his strength didn't do him any good. Daisy was there to meet him as he jumped down to the deck. She let him have it with her belaying pin and he dropped like a felled tree.

"Bill? Bill?" his friends called. "You all right, Bill? Damn him, he's gone to get the money for himself — he didn't throw the rope back — we'll get him — find another rope, no, find a plank — "

Someone else ran and jumped and this one made it, but Mr. Haywood took care of him. It took two taps to down him, but he gave up, just like the first. And Minnie downed the third one.

By this time the Ducks had found planks enough to bridge the short distance, but as the first two started across Pa and Daisy together gave the board a mighty push and they fell over the side with more splashing.

"Burn 'em, the devils! They're there! They're there somewhere — set the boat afire, we'll smoke 'em out! No, No, we'll lose the money. We'll grab 'em and choke it out of 'em — "

The shouts, the glare, the sizzling torches flung across from the *Orpheus*, a burning mast that fell

218

and crashed across their deck — the noise and confusion was terrible. Minnie threw her bucket of water on the flames, but much more water was needed. Farther down the deck, close to the bow, someone with a cooler head had laid a plank across and some of the Sydney Ducks had almost reached the railing. Pa raced down the deck. "Stop right there!" he shouted. "Stop, or I'll shoot!" They hesitated and then came on ahead.

Minnie held her breath. Pa was an excellent shot, but it was dark —

"Stop!" he warned again, and again they advanced one cautious step or two. He took careful aim, and winged the first one. The man grabbed at his leg and toppled off the plank. The next shot got a Duck in the upper arm, and he, too, went down. The rest shrieked and turned, and in the scuffle to go back, two more fell into the water. The profanity was unbelievable, and Daisy said, "Minnie, don't listen!" There was no way to shut it out, though. Even over the furious splashing and floundering, it was impossible not to hear what they were shouting.

Pa called out, "Listen to me, all of you! Get those men out of the water before they drown, and then leave! Get out of here! And don't come back, or next time I'll shoot to kill!"

He leaned over the rail and shouted to the Ducks milling about on the wharf below, "You heard me, now git, or I'll plug you all full of holes!" Minnie could heard quick exchanges, shouts, and then the sound of feet pounding on the street. Their drunken bravado faded fast, and it sounded as if they were falling all over themselves to get away.

The men in the water had been thrown spars and barrels and apparently had splashed their way to safety. Occasionally part of the *Orpheus* flared up and crashed off into the water with frightening hissing and sputtering.

"Glad I lowered all those sails or we might catch on fire, too." It was Tom's cheerful, matter-of-fact voice behind her, and Minnie jumped, startled. "Tom! Where — "

"I tied up the dinghy out there, made her fast to a marker. Come daylight we'll haul her in and unload again, and nothing's even been splashed. Gee, I'm sorry I missed all the fun. But let's keep on hauling water and soaking the deck. The *Venture* might catch even yet."

It was hard to believe that so much had happened in a very few short minutes. They could hardly comprehend that the danger was past, that they were safe. Pa and Mr. Haywood stood at the rail peering out into the flickering eerie light until they were satisfied that not one Duck was still lurking. When Dan Lawrence called out of the darkness they were able to assure him that everything was under control. They lowered the rope ladder and he hurried up, after sending one group of his men off to follow the Ducks.

"Chase them off into the hills," he ordered, "into the next valley if necessary. Don't let them back into those shacks. We'll clean them out of here. And six of you come up here and get rid of these three slugs. They're out as cold as bonitas."

Daisy and Tom and Minnie kept hauling water, bucket after bucket of it, until every inch of the *Venture* deck was as soaked as if there had been a rainstorm. Only then did they feel that they could rest and listen to what Mr. Lawrence and Pierce Weldon and Mr. Haywood were saying.

"If all of us get together, really get together, not just talk about it, appoint men who can't be bribed or scared," Pa was saying earnestly, and Mr. Haywood and Mr. Lawrence were agreeing.

"But," said Dan Lawrence, "we can't do it tonight, or rather this morning, for it's almost dawn. If you're sure you're all all right, get some sleep, and we'll see then what must be done. I'll leave a couple of my men here to keep an eye on things. A bunch of them are already sluicing down the *Orpheus*."

Pa started to protest that it wouldn't be necessary, that he could stay up a while longer. Mr. Lawrence laughed.

"You've been hero enough for one night, Weldon. Ridley and Jones can hang around for a couple of hours, won't hurt them a bit." Then he said a strange thing. "You're a good man, Weldon. If she won't have me, then I'm glad you're the one she's chosen. Probably wouldn't do for a gambler to be a settled married man anyway."

In the darkness beside her Minnie heard Daisy gasp, but she was too tired to wonder what that meant. She was too tired to do anything but stumble toward the companionway and fall sleepily into bed.

20

THE NEXT MORNING was a confusing one. Tom slept several hours and then woke early to swim out to the dinghy and row it back in. He and Pa unloaded it, and after Daisy sent him below to put on some dry clothes, she and Minnie tried to get some order out of the jumble of belongings.

They were all tired, and a little cross. The exhilaration of outwitting the Ducks had faded, leaving them sobered and weary. It was depressing to look over at the *Orpheus*, with her blackened stumps of masts and partly burned-away decking. Minnie shuddered when she thought how easily the same thing could have happened to the *Golden Venture*.

The men Dan Lawrence had detailed to the *Orpheus* had smothered the embers and prevented more damage before they left at daylight. They went yawning back to their rooms behind the Red Rooster. It had been a hard night's work for cardplayers and croupiers who were used to nothing more strenuous than a night at a gaming table.

Minnie and Daisy had fallen asleep without even undressing, and sunrise found them mussed and bedraggled. Daisy, who was always so crisp and starched and shiny-clean, had a sooty smudge across her cheek and her blue dress was rumpled and soiled and had a big tear at the hem.

"I'll clean up later," she said wearily, "but first we'll have to straighten out this mess before we can even think about breakfast."

"Don't worry about a thing, Miss Daisy," said Pa. He sounded surprisingly chipper. "You just sit and rest while I sort out the dishes and edibles."

"Rest?" Daisy was surprised. "You're the one who should be resting. After all, it's not so long since you were very sick. Please, you sit down."

"Both of you sit down and shut up your fussing," ordered Mr. Haywood. "Me'n the children can do this as well as either of you. Minnie, start taking these books back to Daisy's bookshelf — she can line 'em up to suit herself later. Now, do as I say, Daisy, and no back talk."

She sat down again by Pa's side, unable to argue with the old man.

"I may not be the brightest one here, but I'm the oldest and that gives me some rights, don't it?"

Daisy and Pa had to laugh, he was so indignant.

"Besides, you two got other things to get settled, so get at it and let's not waste time."

"What things?" asked Tom.

"Important things like when they'll get married, for one. Now look smart, boy, and don't drop that crock after I risked my life to save it. Get on with your work and don't let your mouth hang open like that. You too, Minnie."

Minnie and Tom ignored his orders and turned to look at the two on the sofa. "Married!" they both shouted. "Married!"

Daisy was first startled and then bright pink with embarrassment. "Mr. Haywood, how could you?" she asked, sounding very close to tears.

Pa seemed surprised, too, but very pleased.

"Will you, Miss Daisy? Will you have me, with all my faults, and hardly two pennies to rub together?"

"Oh, Daisy, please say yes," pleaded Minnie.

"Say yes!" commanded Tom. "It's a wonderful idea."

"I think you're all dreadful," she said, her voice breaking. "It's too serious a matter to joke about!" She wiped away her tears with the hem of her dress and only spread the smudge farther over her face.

Pa said softly, "You're right, Miss Daisy. It is serious, but I'm not joking. Could you possibly consider it? Could you take us, Minnie and me?" He took her grubby hands in his grubby hands. "Will you at least think about it?"

She was laughing and crying at the same time, and her answer came out in a hiccup. "I — I don't know — " Then they all crowded around, Minnie saying, "Daisy, please do! I'd love you for my mother!"

"Daisy, if you don't you're a blasted fool!" shouted Mr. Haywood.

"Daisy, say yes, say yes!" begged Tom.

She pulled herself together and stood up. "I won't say a thing without giving it some thought, and I'll thank you all to let me make up my own mind. Tom, give me those books, you're dropping them all over." She started down the deck toward her cabin. "Mr. Haywood, I'll deal with you later."

"Sounds just like a bloomin' schoolteacher," said Mr. Haywood gloomily. They could hear the cabin door slam shut with considerable force. Pa said sadly, "I didn't handle it right. Now she's mad at all of us."

"Give her a chance to get un-mad, then," said Mr. Haywood. "And don't you all go blamin' me. I just got tired of all this shilly-shallying around, lookin' at each other moon-eyed and not sayin' anything. I like folks to speak out, y'know." Mr. Haywood was grumbling away as usual. "And she's not the only one who has a right to speak out, neither. Women! Contrary things! Try to do them a favor and they turn on you."

"That's not fair, Mr. Haywood!" Minnie turned on him, too. "Nobody wants to be proposed to before she's had a chance to brush her hair."

"Like I said, women! Now be about your business, you two. Tom, get the fire started for breakfast, and then you kids bring more water. I flung the drinkin' water on the hatch cover when it started to burn. And you get cleaned up, Pierce. No woman wants to be proposed to by a man who needs his face washed."

"How come you never married, if you know so

226

much about it?" asked Pa. But he hurried off to take Mr. Haywood's advice. Before long he was back, brushed and combed and wearing a clean shirt. Very soon Daisy came up, too. Her second best work dress was covered with a spotless pinafore, the lace-edged one she usually wore on Sunday. She had pulled her hair up in a firm topknot, but as usual small tendrils had come loose and curled around her forehead and cheeks. And those cheeks were very pink, both from scrubbing and emotion.

While they were gone, Mr. Haywood had bustled about, rearranging and slanting the sail awning so sharply that it made a kind of screen, hiding the sofa and the little area they called their parlor.

"The kitchen help doesn't have to have such a good view of the parlor," he fussed, "and don't you two go peeking, neither. If we spoil this chance we might not get another, Daisy's that stubborn."

Breakfast was not a very lively meal. Pa and Daisy said very little, except for an occasional shy request for the salt, or more bread. Tom and Minnie watched them, fascinated, and neither of them said anything, either, unless Mr. Haywood poked them under the table. He tried to keep up a flow of talk, but no one paid much attention to him. At last they were finished, and he said crossly, "Go set awhile, for mercy's sake, and enjoy the view, if you can't think of anything to talk about. Not you, Tom and Minnie, you stay right here and help me with the dishes."

"Washing dishes is woman's work," objected Tom.

227

"Then you'll do woman's work and no complaints, neither. Women was doin' men's work last night. Minnie and Daisy downed a Duck apiece as good as any man, I seem to recall. Step lively, now, and keep your mind on your work."

Tom didn't really mind helping with the dishes. His objection was just an excuse to see what was going on behind the awning. But under Mr. Haywood's stern direction he and Minnie straightened up the kitchen area without ever once looking toward the "parlor."

"Now you two be as good as your word," Mr. Haywood warned.

"I don't recall that I gave my word to anything," said Minnie innocently.

"I gave it for you. Now you two go below and straighten up the storeroom. I've got to go down and tell the customers the bakery is closed for the day. Oh, I'll be the one as has to hear all the complaints and arguments and hollerin', like always. Why always me?"

He didn't wait for an answer. He tossed the rope ladder over the side and backed down, grumbling all the way to the wharf.

Whatever was said in the parlor, Minnie and Tom never knew, but it was evidently very satisfactory, for soon Pa and Daisy came out from behind the awning smiling.

"She's said yes," said Pa. "Miss Daisy has said yes!"

Then there *was* a celebration. Mr. Haywood

228

shouted to the customers who had been standing patiently in line, "No time for you folks now! Got to drink a toast!" He was so pleased that he added recklessly, "Come back tomorrow and there'll be free hardtack all around!" He immediately regretted this generous offer, but as he said later, "It ain't every day we have a betrothal in the family."

They were toasting the happy couple in water and pretending it was champagne when Dan Lawrence came up the ladder with the mail.

"I called," he said, "but no one heard me. What's going on? Are you celebrating the rout of the Sydney Ducks?"

"Better than that, Mr. Lawrence. Mr. Weldon and I are going to be married!"

"It couldn't happen to two nicer people," he said generously. "I wish both of you all the happiness in the world. When? What are your plans?"

"We really haven't made any yet," said Pa. "I guess I wanted to be sure she wouldn't back out before we started to make plans and I had to admit we'd be starting all over from nothing."

Daisy's usually shining smile was absolutely radiant.

"I won't back out, Pierce Weldon, and I won't mind at all starting over. You and Minnie and I can work together to make our fortune."

"You've got something better than a fortune right now," said Mr. Lawrence quietly and a little sadly. "You have a happy life in store for you. And now, an engagement gift for you, Minnie, my girl. A letter from St. Joseph, Missouri."

Minnie was so pleased that even a long complaining letter from Aunt Addie couldn't spoil her day. She tore it open and skimmed through it rapidly.

"She says she's fine and hopes we are, too, although she doubts it, in this nest of iniquity — what's iniquity, Daisy? — and disease, this city of wickedness and greed. The chickens are laying well, the stable is prospering and Mr. Tinker has finally buckled down to some good hard work — poor Addie Tinker — and Aunt Addie is going to — Oh my goodness! Listen to this! Aunt Addie is going to marry Banker Hanlon as soon as Pierce gives up this gold nonsense and comes back to take over the house because she certainly doesn't need it, not with Mr. Hanlon's house being so much larger and elegant, and what on earth will she do with all that furniture? Pa! Aunt Addie is going to marry Banker Hanlon! We've got our freedom! We've got our freedom!"

They shared another round of toasts to Aunt Addie, to Aunt Addie's future husband, and then Pa said, "Well, Miss Daisy darling, it seems you have a choice. Which will it be? St. Joe and a house already built and furnished, or do we stay and bring San Francisco around to our way of thinking?"

"It's not my choice alone," she answered. "Minnie, what do you think?"

Minnie wrinkled her forehead in thought. This was a serious decision to make. She thought about

231

St. Joe, pleasant, established, old friends and familiar possessions; and San Francisco, new and raw and rough and needing to be tamed. After a long while she finally said, "It takes a power of dusting and waxing to keep that fancy Philadelphia furniture nice, and anyway I think it would be fair if Daisy got to choose her own furniture. Why can't we build a nice little house up on one of the hills here where we can see the sunsets, with room for Tom and Captain Cavendish when they get in to port? We can have a livery stable and a school, too. Folks'll always be needing a school and mules and horses. I vote to settle here."

Daisy hugged her. "That's my choice, too. So there you are, Mr. Weldon, dear, it looks as if you are going to be Californian whether you like it or not."

"I like it fine," he beamed. "Just fine."